"What's going on?"

Karissa looked up at her protector.

Hunter's bearded face had hardened into a fierce mask. "They're burning the cabin. If anyone is alive in here, they expect us to run out where they can pick us off like tin ducks in a county fair target-shooting booth."

Karissa sucked in a breath. "What are we going to do?"

"Not what they expect." He tugged back a corner of the thin area rug they were squatting on, exposing a portion of a trap door.

"Of course! You have a cellar."

Would the smoke penetrate the cellar? Or would the floorboards currently beneath her feet fall in on them, consuming them in flaming debris? Did she want to die in a hole like a rat?

Karissa met the stranger's steel-gray gaze.

"Trust me," he said, voice low and steady, like a rock of dependability...which didn't match his appearance at all.

What choice did she have but to trust him?

Jill Elizabeth Nelson writes what she likes to read—faith-based tales of adventure seasoned with romance. Parts of the year find her and her husband on the international mission field. Other parts find them at home in rural Minnesota, surrounded by the woods and prairie and four grown children and young grandchildren. More about Jill and her books can be found at jillelizabethnelson.com or Facebook.com/jillelizabethnelson.author.

Books by Jill Elizabeth Nelson

Love Inspired Suspense

Evidence of Murder
Witness to Murder
Calculated Revenge
Legacy of Lies
Betrayal on the Border
Frame-Up
Shake Down
Rocky Mountain Sabotage
Duty to Defend
Lone Survivor

Visit the Author Profile page at Harlequin.com.

LONE SURVIVOR

JILL ELIZABETH NELSON

HARLEQUIN® LOVE INSPIRED® SUSPENSE

Recycling programs
for this product may
not exist in your area.

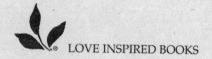 LOVE INSPIRED BOOKS

ISBN-13: 978-1-335-40257-8

Lone Survivor

www.Harlequin.com

Printed in U.S.A.

A father of the fatherless...is God in his holy habitation.
—*Psalm* 68:5

To all those who struggle with the sense of being orphaned and alone in this world. You are not alone, and God will never abandon you.

ONE

Karissa Landon gnawed her lower lip as she guided her compact sedan up the steep gravel driveway toward her cousin Nikki's home in the Cascade Mountains of Oregon. As excited as she'd been to reconnect with this long-lost relative—pretty much the last one on the bare branches of her family tree—now that she was at the moment of truth, her palms were sweating and her heart rate stuttered like she was about to undergo a particularly grueling job interview. Karissa and her cousin had both recently crossed the threshold of thirty years old, and it had been twenty-two years since they'd last seen each other. Would they like the adults the other had become?

Karissa and her twin sister, Anissa, had been inseparable with Nikki when their families lived next door to each other during their early grade school years, but after their families moved far apart, they'd gradually fallen out of touch. Now, this reunion meant a lot to Karissa—probably too much—which led to her arriving at her cousin's place a good half hour earlier than their agreed-upon time. But with her parents and her twin sister gone from this world, she longed for connection with someone who shared her DNA.

She stopped the car at the edge of a circular drive in front of a log house. The structure was considerably bigger and more elaborate than Nikki's reference to it as a "cabin" would have implied during their initial telephone conversation several days ago. Her cousin had sounded delighted to hear from her and fascinated to learn that Karissa had joined an ancestry website specifically to find any remaining relatives. Nikki had been excited to share about her three-month-old son, Kyle, but sad over her husband's recent death due to prostate cancer.

Karissa's insides knotted. Was it unrealistic of her to hope that she and Nikki would rebond after all these years? Regardless, she had to try.

Sucking in a fortifying breath, Karissa stepped out of her car and walked up the three steps onto a wide front porch populated by small tables and chairs, as well as a swing at the far end. The large front door was a unique blend of ornate and rustic. Massive, floor-to-ceiling picture windows to the right of the door suggested a great room that would offer a panoramic vista of the wooded valley below. No wonder her cousin delighted in the place.

Resolute, she knocked on the solid wood and waited…and waited. Not a sound carried to her from the interior. Had her cousin forgotten she was coming? Or maybe Nikki had run out on an errand and would soon be back at the time they'd agreed to meet. Probably that was it. So much for her puppylike eagerness to get this reunion underway.

However, with this view to admire and fresh pine air to invigorate her senses, waiting on the front porch would be no hardship. Karissa stepped toward a chair but halted in front of the windows. The curtains were wide-open, revealing a great room with a vaulted ceiling. The room was tastefully furnished with high-end, rustic-chic furniture. However, it wasn't the loveliness of the space that snared her attention. Her gaze locked onto a pair of bare, feminine feet and legs poking out from behind the brown leather sofa.

Something was wrong. Had her cousin fallen? Was she hurt?

Karissa whirled and raced back to the door. She turned the knob. Thankfully, the door was not locked. She burst inside and rushed toward the woman on the floor then pulled up short with a thin shriek. Nikki lay sprawled on her back, slender arms flung above her head. Her long brown hair fanned out across the cabin floor, the color nearly blending with the medium-toned wood.

"Nikki?" The cry came out hoarse and strangled as Karissa dropped to her knees and felt for a pulse in her cousin's neck. Stupid, futile gesture. There was no life to be found.

Swallowing hard, Karissa squeezed her eyes shut. Surely, this moment was a dream—or rather, a nightmare. Would she wake up soon? She opened her eyes, but the grim reality remained the same. Worse, if there was a *worse* in such a situation, it wasn't even possible to believe that the death was due to natural causes—not with the neat, round bullet hole in the middle of Nikki's forehead. Her cousin had been shot!

Who did this to you, Nikki? Is the killer still in the house?

Karissa's stomach lurched, and she froze in place. Her gaze darted around the vast space. All appeared to be benignly normal—except for a real estate flyer on the floor nearby. With her senses in heightened awareness, the bold black words smacked her between the eyes: Buying or Selling, You Need Marshall Siebender and Associates on Your Team. Strange. Nicki hadn't mentioned letting go of the place. Quite the opposite, in fact.

Focus, girl! Karissa snarled at herself.

She needed to know she was alone in this house. Emptiness and silence met Karissa's senses, but that didn't mean a murderer wasn't lurking somewhere on the premises. The hairs on her arms and the back of her neck stood to attention. She needed to get out of here.

Gripping the back of the couch, Karissa wobbled to her feet. On jellied legs, she managed only a lurching stagger in the direction of the door.

She needed to call the police or the sheriff or whoever handled crime this deep in the boonies. Karissa pulled her cell phone from her handbag and frowned at the screen. No signal. *Great!*

Gazing around, she spotted a landline telephone on the wall above the kitchen peninsula. Karissa rushed to it and snatch up the handset. No dial tone. Her insides went hollow. Now what?

Next best thing—get out of here right now, jump into her car and drive as fast as she could to the nearest law enforcement office. The physical paralysis ebbed, and she accelerated toward the front door. But as her hand closed around the doorknob, a sound arrested her. A soft, mewling cry came from somewhere up the hallway toward the back of the house. The sound escalated into an infant's distinctive wail.

Baby Kyle. How could she have forgotten the child?

Karissa dropped her handbag on a small table next to the door and charged up the hallway. She would get that baby and go. It wasn't like she could leave him here unattended for an indefinite period of time. Besides, as scary as this whole situation was, common sense suggested that the murderer was likely as far away from here as he or she could get by now. What killer shot someone then waited around to get caught? Karissa was going to have to lean into that thought, because a child needed her to be brave right now.

Guided by the infant's howls, Karissa opened the door at the end of the hallway. Late-afternoon sunlight trickled between slight gaps in the curtain panels that covered two windows, allowing her a twilit view of a crib along the left-hand wall and its fussing, kicking occupant. A pang gripped Karissa's middle. Poor, sweet baby. The little guy would never get to know his mother. Or his father, for that matter. Tears stung the backs of Karissa's eyes, but she swallowed them away and marched toward the crib.

Forcing a smile, contrary to her knotted insides, she gazed down at the flailing infant. Did the child somehow sense that pitching a fit was appropriate behavior at the moment? Of course not. Karissa's imagination was running away with her. She picked up the child and cuddled the squirming bundle close. The howling instantly toned down to a thin whine.

"I've got you, sweetie," Karissa murmured as she whirled and headed out of the room.

Her foot kicked something soft, and she looked down to spot the infant's diaper bag. Without a second thought, she bent, hooked the strap over her arm and continued her retreat with barely a hitch in her stride. When she got herself and Kyle to safety, it would be good to have a few of his things along.

Nearly to the front door, a sound halted her—a vehicle approaching up the driveway. Friend or foe? Barely daring to breathe, Karissa darted to the picture window and peered out. A black, four-door pickup truck crunched gravel beneath its tires. Suddenly the vehicle accelerated. No doubt the driver had noticed her little Toyota sitting under the shade of a maple tree that flanked the drive. The extreme reaction didn't bode well. Was the killer returning to the scene of the crime? Why? To grab Kyle or do him harm?

Over her dead body! A possible outcome if this was the killer returning for some nefarious reason. Karissa's breathing hitched.

The truck skidded to a halt, the driver's door sprang open and a male figure jumped out. He had black hair and a sharp beak of a nose, but Karissa's attention was caught by something else. The rays of the westering sun gleamed from the metal object in his hand. A gun! Her mouth went stone dry. Her dead-body vow might soon come true if she didn't get out of this house right now. Making a break for her car was out of the question. The only route left open was out the back door and into the woods.

The baby let out a squawk and kicked her in the

ribs. Karissa looked down. She was squeezing him too tightly. Loosening her hold a bit, she dashed for the rear door. Hand on the knob, she looked back over her shoulder. Her handbag sat on the table next to the door. A heavy footfall on the front porch boards alerted her that she had no time to go back for it. She darted outside with her precious cargo and closed it after her in rapid silence. Tiptoe running, she headed down the deck stairs onto the lawn. If the killer thought she was still in the house, he might waste time looking for her. They would need every second to make the cover of the woods.

Clutching Kyle to her chest, praying he would not cry out, she took off across the lawn. Good thing she was wearing cross-trainers and casual capris, not the skirt she'd almost put on this morning. Even so, her legs couldn't seem to move fast enough. If only they pumped as rapidly as her heart. Or if only Nikki had a smaller backyard.

When she was two-thirds of the way across the grass, a masculine shout from the direction of the house let her know she'd been discovered. Electricity spurted through Karissa's body, and her legs suddenly found new speed. Her breathing rasped in her lungs, and the diaper bag beat a tattoo against her thigh. A sound like a coughing spit rang out, and heat seared her right arm. Crouching low, Karissa burst through a loose-knit set of bushes and scuttled into the shelter of the trees. Another spit sounded, and a small branch next to her head snapped in two.

The killer was using a silencer on his pistol? Did that mean there were neighbors nearby that the shooter didn't want to alert?

Oh, please, God, let it be so...and help me find them.

Karissa kept running, dodging tree trunks, leaping over roots and fallen branches. Her arms wrapped the baby close to her chest, shielding him with her body. But if the shooter knew his way around these woods, she and this infant who depended upon her would be easy prey.

Hunter Raines swung the ax toward the chunk of wood perched atop the chopping block. Beneath his light T-shirt, the muscles along his shoulders, arms and back bunched and flexed with only mild discomfort from the burn scars that ran down the left side of his torso. *Thunk!* The satisfying sound echoed deep in his gut. His lungs sucked in a pine-laden breath as he brought the ax high again and swung it downward. *Thunk!*

A light wind sighed through the branches of the Douglas firs hugging the forest service's two-room cabin he'd occupied for many months now. Birdsong tickled his ears, soothing his senses. No sight or sound of human habitation intruded on the serenity—well, except for the rhythmic thud of his own ax, but he'd soon be done with the humble chore.

How thankful he was for this secluded retreat in the Cascade Mountains offered to him by his forest-ranger brother, Jace. He couldn't think of a better spot to hunker down after his eleven months of torturous skin grafts and therapy and give his wounds—both inner and outer—time to heal. Even now, after more than a year here in the wild, the thought of returning to the claustrophobic beehive of city life in Portland turned him cold.

Yep, he owed Jace big-time for pulling strings to allow him to hole up for a while in this ranger cabin on the edge of Umpqua National Forest. Officially, Hunter was a temporary forest service volunteer tasked with fire watching from the nearby fire tower. Unofficially but more genuinely, he was a heartsick, wounded ex-firefighter struggling to make peace with senseless tragedy.

"Help!"

The plaintive female cry halted Hunter's ax in mid-swing. His heart rate kicked into overdrive. Quivering, he lowered the ax, which then slipped from sweat-slicked palms. Another flashback from the woman's death. Auditory this time. He gulped as blackness edged his vision. *Easy now. Just breathe.* He would *not* give in to another panic attack.

"Help me!"

The cry came again. Closer this time. Not a trick of his wounded mind.

Hunter whirled toward the northern tree line. A slight figure, laden with a bundle hugged to her chest and a large bag dangling from the crook of her arm, staggered toward him. The woman was dressed in casual clothes and sneakers, not hiking garb appropriate to this outdoor recreation area. Long, flame-red hair fluttered around her face, obscuring her features. A wail suddenly erupted from the bundle in the woman's arms.

Hunter's jaw dropped. What was a woman with a baby doing in the back side of nowhere yelling to him for help? If any road but a dirt track led to this area of the forest, he'd guess maybe a vehicle breakdown. Sure, a couple of miles away, beyond the perimeter of federal land, stood a few private houses owned by the elite who could afford fancy mountain getaway homes, but if that's where she originated and she was for some reason without a vehicle, why had she headed deeper into the forest rather than toward the nearest highway? Whatever the reason, it couldn't be good.

The woman tottered nearer. Her heaving breaths and whimpers betrayed stark terror. But it was the redness dripping down the woman's arm and plinking in drops from her bent elbow that jolted Hunter out of inertia— a paralysis that would never have gripped him in the face of emergency in his Before Incident days. Mentally slapping himself, Hunter strode toward the woman and child.

"What's going on?" He reached her just as her knees buckled.

With an exclamation, he caught her and her tiny cargo and lowered them both to the ground. The woman sat blinking at him through a veil of pine needle–strewn hair that blocked him from getting a good look at her face. Her mouth worked like she wanted to speak but couldn't find the words. His hand around her upper arm was sticky with her blood.

"You're hurt. Let's get a look at the wound."

"N-no." She inhaled a loud, raspy breath. "I—I think it's just a scratch."

"A lot of blood for just a scratch."

"Call the sheriff!" Her voice came out a thin screech. "That's all I want you to do. Get someone up here. My cousin's been murdered." Her voice lowered to a hoarse whisper. "I meant to surprise her by arriving earlier than expected. I thought it would be so much fun." She choked on a sob. "But I found her shot d-dead. Then the baby started crying, and I grabbed him and then the killer came back before I could leave in my car, so I ran away, but the killer shot at us, and I've been running for miles, and…" Her flood of words trailed away between quivering lips.

A soft wail from the infant punctuated the sudden silence.

Hunter's jaw hardened. The tale was completely wild, but if that was truly a bullet wound in her arm then he needed to believe her and take action. "Let's get you inside first." In the relative safety of the cabin, he could examine her injury and verify or disprove her story.

She nodded wordlessly.

"Can I take the child?"

She stiffened and pulled away from him, clutching her bundle. The little one kicked and fussed.

Hunter raised his hands, palms out, in a nonthreatening gesture. "Easy there. You're safe now."

She slumped toward him, and with a gentleness that contradicted the knots around his insides, Hunter helped her up. With him lending significant support, they made it onto the wooden porch. She was a petite thing, dwarfed by him, but she had an athletic build, evidently no couch potato, based on her ability to run miles while wounded and carrying a baby. First thing would be to triage that wound. Then he'd know whether to call for help or treat the injury first.

His training was starting to kick in, for whatever meager satisfaction *that* knowledge offered. It hadn't saved the woman who'd depended on him before… No. He couldn't go there. Not now. Not when he was once again thrust into a situation where lives depended on him. If a killer really was on the trail of this woman and her baby, he had to keep them safe or he might as well die trying. He'd never survive another failure.

Inside the cabin, Hunter guided her to the cushioned sofa. She sank onto it and began cooing to the baby and tickling his plump cheeks, which dialed the fussing back to a thin whine. Of course, the child could be a girl, but the blue sleeper with a train embroidered over the right breast suggested a boy. From this vantage point, gazing down at the top of the woman's head as she focused on the child, he still couldn't see her face, but he made out an angry red streak oozing blood on her upper bicep area where the short sleeve of her blouse was ripped. Could have been caused by a branch while running through the forest, but that sort of wound would likely be more ragged and contain debris. This wound was clean and straight—just like a bullet graze sustained from a distance. A burn settled deep in his belly. Some lowlife took a shot at a woman holding a baby.

The wound could wait a few more minutes. He turned on the heels of his hiking boots and tromped across the plank flooring to the two-way radio on his desk at the far side of the room.

"Let's call for help," he said. "Then we'll get that wound cleaned and bandaged."

"Please, yes." Her assent carried to him in shaken tones.

The radio frequency was preset to the main park station, where his brother worked. Jace would be able to get law enforcement and emergency services up here ASAP. Hunter keyed the mic and put in the call.

"Umpqua Ranger Station," a male voice answered. "Remy Nolan speaking."

Hunter let out a grunt under his breath. Not his brother. A ranger Hunter hadn't met yet? He thought he'd met them all. Must be a new hire. Hunter identified himself as Jace's brother, gave his location and then tersely described his issue with the woman and child. Stone silence answered him for several heartbeats.

"Say again?" the man said. "No, never mind. I heard you. I'm just processing this strangeness on top of strangeness."

"Why? What's going on?"

"There's been a bomb threat at the North Umpqua Hydroelectric Project. Everyone and their bomb-sniffing dog is there now, including Jace."

Hunter's heart lurched. He swallowed against a dry mouth. Jace would be okay. He had to believe that.

"That's not the kind of danger a forest ranger finds himself in every day," he told Remy. "I'll sure be keeping them in my prayers, but right now, we need emergency services to pick up the woman and baby. All I've got for transportation is a motorcycle, and that won't do for them."

"Understood. I'll scramble someone as soon as I can."

"And send investigators to my cousin's place," said a soft female voice over Hunter's shoulder.

"What's that address?" the ranger answered.

The woman rattled off an address that would put it among the expensive residences just outside the park borders.

"And your name?"

The woman spoke a name Hunter had hoped never to hear again. A chill rippled across his flesh, raising the hairs on his arms and neck. Karissa Landon? Anissa's twin sister? It couldn't be!

God, You wouldn't do that to me, would you?

As if moving through clotted mud, Hunter slowly swiveled, and for the first time, he looked full into the woman's face, cleared of its veil of hair and forest debris. His heart came to a full stop then stumbled into a gallop. He found himself peering into the same vivid green eyes that haunted his nightmares. Eyes that pleaded with him to save her. Eyes that belonged to a dead woman. This one's twin. The woman he'd failed to rescue from the fire that ended his career as a Portland firefighter.

How long did he have before Karissa recalled the media coverage, including an unflattering photo of him, and figured out who he was now that she had obviously calmed? Seconds? He braced himself.

But she merely blinked at him, neutral expression morphing into puzzlement. "Are you all right? You suddenly lost half your tan."

Hunter searched for his voice. Karissa clearly didn't recognize him. Of course, they'd never met in person, but his picture had been well publicized not long after the horrible tragedy. He'd been clean shaven in those shots, though, and his hair had been short. Now, with a full beard and hair that hadn't seen scissors in months, not to mention his scars, he probably looked like some kind of holdover from the Gold Rush days. However, he couldn't count on facial hair to maintain his camouflage indefinitely. At any moment, she would recognize who he was, and she would despise him. Probably as soon as she asked him to introduce himself. He'd put that moment off as long as possible.

"You two still there?" The ranger's query from the other end of the radio snapped Hunter back into the moment.

"Ten-four, Remy. We'll be here waiting for the cavalry to show up." How had his voice come out so upbeat when panic sought to devour him alive?

"Hang tight. Over and out." The airwaves went dead.

Hunter got up and went for his gun case. He took out the rifle, loaded it, made sure the safety was on and then propped the firearm against his desk. A strangled noise coming from his female houseguest drew his attention. Had she recognized him at last? Stiffening, Hunter forced himself to turn toward Karissa. She wasn't staring at him, but at his gun.

"How did life suddenly turn so dangerous we might actually have to use that to defend ourselves?" Her hoarse whisper barely carried to him over the fussing of the baby, who was kicking and flailing on the hearth rug.

He lifted one side of his mouth in a grim half smile. "We'll be ready if we have unwelcome intruders before help arrives."

The tension around her lips eased marginally, and she jerked a nod in his direction.

"Let's get that wound cleaned up," he said and went for his first aid kit.

Soon, he had a bandage on the bullet crease that had nearly ceased bleeding since she was no longer exerting herself. It was impressive that she didn't cry out, just gnawed her lower lip and kept her gaze averted. As soon as he was done with her, Karissa began rummaging in the diaper bag.

"Thank You, Lord." She pulled out a can of powdered formula and glanced over her shoulder at him. "You wouldn't have any purified water, would you? I changed him while you were on the radio, but now this little guy is hungry as a bear. Might as well feed him while we wait."

"I think I can accommodate." Hunter ventured a full smile, but her focus had already left him as she scooped up the baby. The little fellow was now alternating between howls and trying to eat his fist.

A few minutes later, the baby was contentedly guzzling while Karissa held him on the threadbare sofa that served as Hunter's main piece of furniture, other than his bed in the loft, and the steel-topped table where he ate his meals.

Hunter hefted the rifle and kept watch at the window while he prayed for a rescue vehicle to soon emerge from the break in the trees where a one-lane dirt track led into the clearing. In a short while, muted thunder began to grow louder, closing in from a distance. Not thunder. An engine. No—engines, plural, and at least one of them was a diesel. Hunter's insides tensed. Something wasn't right. Too many vehicles to pick up one woman and a baby—especially with a bomb threat on.

A large white SUV with the forest service logo on the side panel burst from the tree line, traveling recklessly fast. A second vehicle—this one a black-as-sin, heavy-duty pickup truck—followed nearly on the SUV's bumper. Both vehicles braked suddenly and skidded to a stop.

What was sticking out through the second vehicle's windows? Waning sunlight reflected off metal. Guns! Pulse rate skyrocketing, Hunter whirled away from the window toward his innocent and oblivious charges.

"We're under attack!" he cried as a fusillade of bullets thudded into the cabin's thick log walls, shattering the window where he'd been standing a split second before.

TWO

Kyle against her shoulder as she worked on burping him, Karissa froze in midpat. Had she heard right? They were being attacked?

Barely had she begun to process the answer when she found herself wrapped in great bear arms. Hugged against a solid chest, she and the baby were half dragged, half carried deep into the kitchen area. The man upended the thick, metal-topped table and thrust her and Kyle down behind its cover.

"Someone's shooting at us." The words exploded from her mouth.

"You think?" he growled. His firm square lips thinned into a pencil line as he trained his rifle barrel around the edge of the table toward the front door.

She glared at her protector as if he were personally responsible for the attack. Ridiculous reaction, but there was no one else to glare at as heat in her gut battled ice in her chest. There had been a couple of tense situations on the mission field in Belize when she'd had opportunity to experience this toxic mix of outrage and terror, and she didn't like it any better now than she had then.

The automatic gunfire lulled then renewed. Karissa cringed at the *thwap* of bullets striking furniture, the tinkle of glass smashing and a sudden spate of metallic gongs as a ribbon of bullets played off the set of pots and pans hanging from ceiling hooks. Kyle thrashed and howled as she cuddled him close. An impact sent the heavy table scooting a few inches backward toward them.

Then the gunfire suddenly ceased. An eerie quietness descended on the cabin. Even the baby seemed to be holding his breath. Then he suddenly stiffened, and his sweet little face screwed up in preparation for renewed howling. Karissa shushed and bounced him. Gradually, his expression relaxed, and he apparently decided sticking his thumb in his mouth was a better alternative to straining his vocal cords.

The cabin owner's intense gray gaze bored into her. "Are you both all right?"

Karissa quickly examined the baby, but he seemed unhurt. In fact, his eyelids appeared to be growing heavy. Poor kid had been through a lot of trauma and excitement that he had no way to understand in the past couple of hours.

"We're good," she said.

"Not yet, we're not. They could burst in here any second to check their handiwork, and my rifle is a poor match for automatic weapons."

A sudden *whoosh* and a crackling noise overhead sent Karissa's gaze toward the ceiling. An acrid smell began teasing Karissa's nostrils.

"What's going on?" She looked up at her protector.

The mountain man's bearded face had hardened into

a fierce mask. "The good news is they don't plan to rush in here. The bad news is they're burning the cabin. If anyone is alive in here, they expect us to run out where they can pick us off like tin ducks in a county fair target-shooting booth."

Karissa sucked in a breath. "What are we going to do?"

"Not what they expect." He turned away from her and tugged back a corner of the thin area rug they were squatting on, exposing a portion of a trapdoor.

"Of course! You have a cellar." Karissa scooted off the rug and allowed him to completely uncover the door.

The man grabbed an iron ring attached to one side of the door and lifted the hatch. Chilly air wafted upward, pebbling the skin on her bare arms. Her wound throbbed. Karissa glanced toward the ceiling, where heat already radiated downward, and then back into the cellar where utter blackness beckoned. Would the smoke penetrate the cellar? Or would the floorboards currently beneath her feet fall in on them, consuming them in flaming debris? Did she want to die in a hole like a rat? What was the alternative?

Karissa met the stranger's steel-gray gaze.

"Trust me," he said, voice low and steady, like a rock of dependability...which didn't match his appearance at all. The shaggy brown hair and beard, along with faded, puckered scars on the left side of his upper cheek and forehead gave the guy a dangerous look—like a true wild mountain man.

What choice did she have but to trust him, regardless of appearance? He'd done nothing but show her kindness, while she'd brought destruction and possible death down upon him. She nodded. He smiled. The gesture softened his forbidding appearance.

"I'll go down first," he said, "and turn on some light. Then you can hand me the baby and come on down yourself. But we have to move quickly. This cabin will burn fast."

How could this guy stay so calm, planning every-thing out neatly in a situation like this? Karissa's shivers had become shakes that threatened to destroy the last of her sanity. The crackles from above were turning into a roar, and heat intensified atop her head.

"Let's do this," she said between gritted teeth.

The man nimbly disappeared into the blackness. Eternal moments later, a dim light came on, and she was gazing into his upturned face. He reached upward, and she handed him the baby. Strange how handing over her little charge of short acquaintance should feel like such a wrench.

"Now you," he said, cradling the baby effortlessly in the crook of an elbow. "I'll steady you if you lose your balance." He offered his free hand.

Gulping, Karissa clambered down the ladder and found her feet on a cement floor. Immediately, the man returned Kyle to her and pulled the cord to bring the trapdoor down. It landed with a loud *whump*, sealing them off from the main floor. The light of a single over-head bulb offered only a dim view of their surround-ings. Not much to see. Cinder-block walls, one side of which hosted a set of shelves that held fruits and veg-etables in sealed canning jars. A long, wooden trough sat against the opposite wall. The black dirt inside it appeared to be the source of the pungent, earthy smell that filled the space that was about half the size of the cabin above.

"Worm farm," her host said with a wry half grin. "I've done a lot of fishing over the past year I've been staying here, courtesy of the forest service."

Karissa frowned. "Is this our big choice? Die down here with the worms when the smoke gets us or the floor collapses on us, or stay above and let the fire take us?"

The man cocked his head at her. "Intelligent questions, but I wouldn't have led us down here if I didn't have a plan for that contingency. Follow me."

He grabbed his rifle and a large flashlight from a nearby shelf and headed toward the corner of the room. There, he opened a metal door that had been hidden from view by the shelving.

"Behold our sanctuary." He motioned beyond the door.

A small laugh, born of strung-out nerves, escaped Karissa's throat as she brushed past him into the dimness of a tunnel. "You are the quintessential oxymoron of a mountain man."

"I'd like to ask you what you mean by that statement, but I think the question will have to wait."

He pulled the thick door closed after them just as a loud crash from above signaled something, probably the roof, collapsing. The baby jerked out of his almost-sleep and started to cry. Karissa bounced him up and down in the comforting grip of both her arms.

"Follow me," her rescuer said and led the way up the tunnel.

The flashlight's beam played eerie shadows across the cinder-block walls. Karissa trembled, as much from tension as the dank chill. At least she could be grateful they weren't caught up in the heat of the flames above.

Shortly, they came to another iron door. Her guide pushed it open. Karissa stepped into a small room set up with several cots, a small table and shelving that held nonperishable food staples and jugs of what appeared to be water. The temperature in the room was still cool, but at least it wasn't dank.

"We're in a bunker," she stated matter-of-factly.

The mountain man placed the lamp on the table and grinned in her direction. "Good observation. We're not even directly under the cabin any longer. This is a shelter in case a forest fire gets out of hand."

"Handy for us."

He chuckled, a mellow sound that soothed her frazzled nerves. "You can say that again. We'll hole up here until darkness falls. Regardless of a bomb threat, the smoke should soon fetch real rangers to the scene, so I don't figure our attackers will hang around long. But if by some chance the real rangers *don't* show up, and our enemies aren't satisfied that we're dead but they're hanging around somewhere to make sure, then darkness is our best cover to help us sneak away."

"Real rangers? You've said those words twice. What do you mean?"

The man frowned. "I'm going to jump to a bit of a conclusion, but the guy we talked to on the radio was no one I knew, and I thought I'd met all the personnel at the park over the past thirteen months that I've been living here. A bomb scare—and hopefully that's all it is—would be just the sort of thing to empty out the main ranger station so that an impostor could sit in and wait for a woman running for her life to show up or reach out for help. I can't think of another way to explain how a truckload of gunmen knew where to come for you less than twenty minutes after our radio call."

The strength suddenly left Karissa's knees, and she plopped onto a wooden chair. "I can't explain it another way, either." Her voice came out as breathless as if she'd just finished her morning jog.

She swallowed against a dry throat as the implications of the attack on them sank in. She'd assumed she was fleeing from a single, desperate murderer who was trying to shut her up about his crime, but a plot that involved a bomb scare, a fake ranger and a posse of killers was a much larger conspiracy run by someone with far-reaching resources and considerable ruthlessness and determination. Clearly, he didn't even draw the line at killing an infant. Suddenly, it seemed that her cousin's murder might be the tip of the proverbial iceberg.

An opened bottle of water appeared under her nose. She blinked, coming out of her daze, and took the bottle from Hunter's hand.

"Thank you." She gulped greedily then inhaled a long breath and let it out in short, quivering puffs. "All right then." She gazed up at her protector's sober face. "I can't thank you enough for being here and knowing what to do. I'm so, so sorry for getting you involved in this."

"What exactly is *this*?" His tone was sharp, and his eyes narrowed on her.

"I wish I knew." Tears stung the backs of Karissa's eyes. "Everything happened just as I told you. I went to visit a cousin I hadn't seen in—well, forever, found her dead, grabbed the baby, ran away from the killer and here I am. I'm asking the same question you are. What in the world is going on?"

His gaze seemed to sift through her, but at last his facial expression relaxed, and he nodded. "No need to apologize or to thank *me*. Thank God. This has to be more than coincidence that you showed up on my doorstep."

An indefinable something in his expression seemed to be trying to communicate a message beyond his words, but Karissa had no idea what that message might be.

"You're a Christian?" she asked.

"Yes." The word was terse in a way that almost negated the answer.

Her rescuer looked away and set about lighting a nearby kerosene lamp, considerably brightening the room. Then he pulled a large rucksack off one of the shelves and plopped it onto a chair by the table. Karissa checked the baby in her arms and found him fast asleep. She gently laid him down on one of the cots.

"I'm a Christian, too," she said. "Fresh off the mission field in Belize, actually."

"Belize?" The man stopped transferring various supplies from the shelving to the rucksack and stared at her. "You've been out of the country? For how long? I mean, what caused you to go there?" The normal deep tone of his voice had morphed upward a few notes, as if the questions pushed through tightened vocal cords.

Karissa's skin prickled as she studied his tense posture. What had suddenly raised this cool-under-pressure Galahad's anxiety level? Shouldn't she try to find out more about this man she was trusting with her and Kyle's lives?

She forced a smile. "A bit late in our strange acquaintance, but may I get your name?"

The man's body went from tense to rigid, and his facial expression became one of someone bracing for a blow. "I'm Hunter Raines." The pronouncement came in a fatalistic tone.

Karissa furrowed her brow. What was the guy trying to tell her without actually telling her? Was the name supposed to mean something to her? Maybe this Hunter Raines had some sort of history that she'd know about if she'd been in the US in the past two years. Maybe she ought to be afraid of him. More afraid than of the killers who had tried to shoot and then incinerate them? Unlikely. Besides, he'd shown every sign of genuine caring and no sign of aggression. She'd lived her life thus far giving people the benefit of the doubt. Why stop now?

She stuck out her hand toward her benefactor. "Hi, I'm Karissa Landon."

Hunter accepted her handshake, his palm rough, his grip strong without being overpowering. "Yes, you said so when we were talking with Remy on the radio, but I appreciate the formal introduction."

His expression had gone from defensive to bewildered. Amazing how little that beard hid his reactions when his eyes were so expressive. An intriguingly rich shade of gray, too. Not that she needed to be noticing something like that in this situation.

"To answer your questions," she said, "I was on the mission field for twenty-four months, living a dream of serving the poor in practical and spiritual ways. I came back three weeks ago on furlough, but, God willing, I plan to return to Belize in a year or so. While I'm Stateside, I wanted to connect with what family I have left…"

The last sentence trailed off as the enormity of her cousin's murder flooded over Karissa once again. Her head drooped as a soft sob choked her.

"We'll get through this." Hunter's voice was gruff. "And we'll find out who did that to your cousin."

Karissa lifted her gaze. "Nobody is promised tomorrow or answers to their questions or even justice. Not in this life. I keep my sanity by clinging to faith that God sees and knows and understands and will bring everything right in the end. If I didn't believe that, my heart would be withered to dust by now."

"You've been through some tough things, huh?"

"You have no idea."

Hunter winced and looked away.

"I sense you've been through a few things yourself," she said.

Karissa barely restrained herself from asking pointblank how he got his scars. But if he answered her question, fair play might make her feel obligated to tell him about her parents' fatal car wreck and her sister's tragic death in a fire, and how going on the mission field had been a sanity saver at a horrible time in her life. These were not things she wanted to discuss with an almost stranger.

However, she couldn't shake the feeling that something about her had this guy spooked, and that sense of something being off spooked *her*. Until she figured out what it was, she was going to have a hard time taking

Hunter Raines—extraordinarily competent and courageous as he obviously was—at face value.

Hunter busied himself with packing the rucksack.
The mundane chore gave him a little space to get his
head together. He put in everything they might need
for a few days of roughing it if they were for some reason unable to reach the destination he had in mind for
them tonight. However, diapers were not something he'd
thought to stock down here, and the closest he could
get to formula was powdered milk. Who knew how the
baby would ingest any milk since his bottle had been
left lying on the side table near the couch and was now
as incinerated as the rest of the furnishings. Hopefully,
they'd find help sooner rather than later and wouldn't
actually be forced to camp out, but he intended to be as
prepared as possible for whatever eventuality.

Was it possible Karissa had never heard of him? She
said she'd been in Belize for two years and had been
back in the States for a few weeks now. The firestorm
of media condemnation hadn't broken over him until at
least ten days after the fire, so it was possible that she'd
buried her sister and left the country before his reputa-
tion had been publicly annihilated. Whether the condemnation was deserved or undeserved, he still wasn't
convinced in his own mind.

Under initial questioning, after he awakened in the
hospital, he'd been so sure that he'd inspected the equipment right before the fire callout, but his initialed checklist was not on the clipboard or in the computer system
like it should have been if he'd actually done it. In his
dazed and suffering state, had he mixed up the memory

of the inspection with the dozens of other times he'd performed that routine task? If his memory was faulty, and he hadn't done the scheduled inspection, then he really was responsible for the equipment failure that led to the death of Karissa's sister and his own serious injury. But if his memory was true, then what happened to the checklist? He had no answers, and the questions continued to torment him worse than his burns ever did.

At least it was a small mercy—well, a rather large one—that she didn't know who he was…for the moment. Her ignorance about him wasn't likely to remain permanent now that she was back in the country. Someone would tell her about him. He'd have to be grateful for whatever reprieve he was given and hope that they were no longer in each other's company when his identity was exposed.

Hunter turned toward the chair where Karissa sat next to the cot watching the sleeping baby. He froze with a sucked-in breath. What was the matter with him? He'd seen women with babies hundreds of times and usually eyed them with a wistful expectation that one day he'd be a family man. Now, with that hope snuffed out by his ugly burns and uglier notoriety, what a cruel joke that the wish-I-had-a-family feeling should hit him like a truck at this moment with this particular woman as she sat smiling down at a sleeping infant that wasn't even hers. The flickering lamplight drew out the warmth in her vivid hair and painted her face with pensive shadows that enhanced the natural beauty of her heart-shaped face, slim nose and delicately formed lips. He couldn't be attracted to her. He would *not* allow that.

She lifted her head, and her green eyes met his gray

ones. The smile was gone. If he had to summarize her expression in one word, he'd say dread.

"Do you think they're still out there…? No, forget that question. You couldn't possibly answer, and it was rhetorical, anyway." Karissa visibly drew herself up straighter. "Thank you once again, by the way, for everything, and I'm really sorry about the loss of your cabin."

"Not my cabin. Belongs to the forest service. They might not be too happy." He lifted one corner of his mouth and shook his head. "I'd like to say 'my pleasure,' but this isn't a pleasant situation. However, I *can* say that I'm glad I was here and able to help."

More than you know. If only he could convince himself that saving her and the baby made up for the death of Karissa's sister. But there was no possible compensation if his negligence had cost a life.

Her gaze traveled the small room. "Is it usual for ranger cabins to come with a bunker in the earth below?"

He forced a smile. "No, it's not. Though after the rousing success of this one, it might become standard practice. I've been living out here over a year as a volunteer fire spotter, and last summer I had this idea about putting one in. Something to do to pass the time. My park-ranger brother got the go-ahead from the powers that be, since the project was going to be on my dime, and we worked on it together."

"He sounds like another hypercompetent guy like you."

Hunter cocked his head. "Is that how I strike you?"

She pursed her lips. "Self-sufficient, for sure, or you

wouldn't live out here on your own." Her gaze on him was shrewd, assessing.

Was she asking him without coming right out and asking him if he was hiding from something? Maybe he was. If only he could hide from himself when the tormenting questions and memories attacked him.

"Here." He handed her an energy bar from his stash. "Better eat this, because we'll be leaving here soon."

Her gaze skimmed the room. "How do we get out?"

He pointed upward. "There's a camouflaged double-hatch opening in the ceiling with a telescoping ladder that will take us outside near the edge of the forest. I'm a little nervous that my brother hasn't shown up and knocked at the top hatch. He may be the only one in the forest service who knows exactly where the hatch is. If the forest service hasn't come by to check on the cabin fire then it's remotely possible our enemies may be observing the clearing for any signs of life. It'll be dusk now, but the darkness will be part of our cover. Stick close to me, and you'll be fine."

"Why don't we just wait a little longer until the good guys arrive to check out the fire? Surely someone will come eventually."

Hunter shook his head. "If the cavalry was going to arrive, it would have done so already—my brother leading the charge." His jaw hardened against the knot in his gut. "It could mean that things escalated at the power station." *Jace, I hope you're all right.*

Karissa reached out and touched his arm. The gentle compassion in her gaze seemed to travel through her fingertips and touch his soul. "You must be so worried."

Hunter rent his gaze away from hers. Of course, she

would feel special sympathy toward someone fearing for a sibling's safety.

He cleared his throat. "When we leave here, we won't be heading for any ranger station or park out-post where hostile eyes might be watching for us. With the resources we've seen displayed so far by whoever is after you, I don't trust approaching just anyone for help. We're in for a long, rather uncomfortable night of walk-ing, but I have a destination in mind. Are you up for it?"

The woman squared her delicate chin and rose to all of her no more than five feet three inches of dainty height. There was nothing dainty or delicate in the flash of those green eyes. "I've marched up mountains, slogged through swamps and chopped my way through jungles. Bring it!"

Warmth rushed through Hunter's chest, and he couldn't swallow his grin. This woman was in a class by herself. "You know what? I believe I'm the one who might have to struggle to keep up."

Karissa jerked a nod and turned away, but not fast enough to hide the small answering grin. She picked up a light blanket and began folding it in an odd way.

"What are you doing?" he asked.

"Making a baby sling for Kyle that will keep my hands free. Belizean women do this all the time."

"Good. The sling will help keep you and him warm, too. It's summer, but the woods at night at this eleva-tion can still be cool."

The intricacies of her sling and how she got the baby into it without waking him up were mysteries to Hunter, but soon they were ready to head up and out. He opened the bottom hatch door and the telescoping ladder slid into place, just reaching the ground at his feet. Above him was a cement tube around four feet wide and about three-quarters his height. He climbed up to the fire-proof upper hatch, but his hand hesitated on the lock.

God, please help us.

Despite his earlier words about their attackers not waiting around for the real rangers to arrive, the fact that those rangers hadn't come set him on edge. Their attackers could still be out there, waiting for them to pop their heads up like gophers. Then again, it was highly improbable that their attackers knew about the bunker. No doubt he was uneasy over nothing. Still, Hunter held his breath as he released the locking mechanism and shoved the hatch open.

Smoke-tinged twilight air washed over him. An owl hooted nearby, and crickets fiddled their tunes. Hunter's shoulders relaxed. If human beings were still lurking around out there, he wouldn't be hearing those sounds.

He looked down at Karissa, who stood directly below, gazing up at him with questions in her eyes. "All clear, I'd say. Hand me the pack, would you?"

Her strained features relaxed, and she complied, handling the heavy article with ease. He thrust the pack, with the rifle strapped to its side, out onto the dew-sprinkled grass and climbed out of the tube after it. Sprightly as a spider monkey, Karissa climbed out after him, evidently not the least hindered by the precious cargo in her sling or her bullet wound.

While he donned the pack, Hunter's gaze roamed the area. About thirty yards away, the remains of his cabin smoldered. Stray sparks winked at him from the burned wood. He suppressed a shudder at the thought of what would have become of all three of them had there been no bunker retreat.

God, were You guiding me with that idea to build one?

At the time, it had seemed like nothing more than a useful way to pass the abundance of time he had on his hands. Of course, if it *had* been an inspired idea, the providential point would have been to protect Karissa and the innocent baby. In surrendering his life to the Lord during the time period he was undergoing physical therapy, he'd been humbly grateful to squeak through the door of salvation for his soul in the next life. He didn't expect or deserve anything more in this one.

"Let's get going," he said to his petite companion and stepped up behind her.

An angry bee zipped past his head. At least that's what it sounded like. His heart squeezed into a fist as his brain kicked out the truth.

Not a bee—a bullet.

Hunter grabbed Karissa and the baby and shoved them ahead of him into the trees.

"Run!"

THREE

How could this be happening again? She and the baby fleeing through the woods from flying bullets. At least she wasn't alone this time. Hunter had taken the lead at what felt like a breakneck pace up and down the hilly terrain. Yet he always seemed to place his feet perfectly, despite the darkness, showing her safe passage around trees and avoiding potholes and forest debris. Karissa's breathing came in sharp gasps, as much from fear as exertion, and the roar of her pulse in her ears held all other sounds at bay.

God, help us!

At last, her guide slowed and then halted near the edge of a moonlit clearing. Karissa stopped next to him, swaying on tingling feet. Every muscle hummed, high on adrenaline. Hunter's hand on her elbow steadied her. The baby let out one of those long infant sighs but seemed, oddly enough, to have slept through the excitement. Probably the rhythmic sway of the sling had lulled him as she ran.

"I hope you know…where we are…because I'm clueless," she puffed out raggedly.

"I have a general idea, and better yet, I know where we're going. Our pursuers don't." His voice came out strained but only mildly breathless. "That may be our best advantage right now, as well as the darkness, though low visibility could work against us also."

Karissa gulped in a long breath of air then let it out slowly. Hands on hips, she stared up at Hunter's strong profile outlined in the moonlight. "How did the shooter see to fire at us? And where was he firing from? I didn't hear the shot."

"I've been mulling over those things, too. A night-vision scope on a high-powered rifle would answer the vision problem, and a silencer would account for lack of sound, as well as why the shooter missed that first critical shot. Silencers can negatively affect accuracy. I suspect the sniper was positioned in the fire tower about a half mile from the cabin. That's why I wasn't alerted to his presence by a disruption in the normal night sounds of the forest."

"But how did they know we might have survived that horrendous fire?"

Hunter's face swiveled toward her. She couldn't read his expression in the dimness, but his eyes bored into her. "As I've said before, you ask good questions. It's possible the fake ranger found the plans for the bunker while he was at the main station and decided to post someone to wait and see if we popped out."

"Why didn't they just lurk and ambush at the opening or come on down there after us right away?"

"As to the former, I doubt they dared hang around the area very long, risking being spotted close to the burned-out cabin by any legitimate park personnel who might have showed up. As to the latter—" his shoulders rolled in a shrug "—I doubt they could find the hatch. It's not where the plans say it should be. Jace and I changed the location at the last minute, intending to update the plans, but I don't remember that either of us got around to doing it. Also, the hatch is very well camouflaged."

Karissa rolled her shoulders in a shrug. "Good explanation, but is this Remy guy calling the shots—literally—or does he have a boss who is behind all of this?"

Hunter grunted. "Either way, it appears whoever is after us has access to tremendous resources and no hesitancy about using them."

"After *us*? Me, you mean. I'm the one who stumbled onto the murder scene. I'm sure he's worried I caught a glimpse of his face. *You* are collateral damage. However, I can't say what intentions the killer had for Kyle, since we don't know the motive behind all this mayhem."

Hunter shook his head. "I'm now as much of a target as you are. Our enemy needs to eliminate anyone you've talked to or anyone who is standing between him and you."

"Again, I'm *so* sorry." A bitter tang flooded her mouth as her stomach twisted.

He shook his head. "God led you to me. I'm as sure of that as my own name. Leave it with Him."

"I'll try. I'm mostly concerned about getting this little guy to safety." She caressed the top of the downy head poking out of the sling under her chin. "Us, too, of course. Will the killers come after us?"

"Possible, but doubtful." Hunter shrugged. "It's extremely difficult to track anyone through the woods in the dark, though I can't rule out night vision goggles if they had a night scope on that rifle. We'll have to hope for the best and hurry on our way."

Her insides unknotted a smidgeon. "Okay, so what's the plan?"

"That long night hike I told you about. If you need a respite we can stop, but only briefly. We've got a lot of ground to cover before sunup. If necessary, I can carry you for a while."

The nonsensical image of him cradling *her like* a baby while she cradled Kyle struck her as ridiculous, and a laugh snorted out her nose.

"Don't like that idea?" He grinned at her, teeth flashing white under the moon's rays.

On the surface, Hunter might look a bit rough around the edges, but he had a very nice smile.

"I don't find it too practical." She squelched the spark of silly attraction.

"It isn't, especially when I need to be light-footed, wary and smart with our route."

"You're not going to tell me our destination?"

The grin flashed once more. "That's where this plan gets good. By dawn, we should arrive at an old disused logging road. If we follow it for a mile or so, we'll end up behind a hole-in-the-wall biker bar."

Her jaw dropped, and he lifted a quieting hand.

"It's not *that* kind of bar. The patrons' idea of an adult beverage is a triple espresso, and the owner heads a gang of Christian bikers who hang out together plotting ways to bless people and minister to other bikers and people experiencing hard times. They'll fall all over themselves to help us."

Karissa jerked her chin in as much of a nod as she could manage without displaying the shakes that quivered her insides. "Okay, let's do this."

"This way." Her guide waved her after him as he headed off.

They walked up small hills and down into miniature vales, never leaving tree cover. Huffing, she struggled to keep up with Hunter's long-legged stride but bit back her complaints because he consistently opened the way for her through the pervasive underbrush and prickly branches. Thankfully, the baby remained asleep. Though the night woods could seem eerie—all strange noises and odors with minimal sight—the darkness also offered a sense of cocooning protection.

They'd been moving steadily for what seemed like hours, but was probably less, when they came to a small burbling stream. On the bank, Hunter held up a hand for a halt.

"Where—" she started, but Hunter shushed her.

He stood very still, head cocked, as if listening intently. Apparently, he heard something he didn't like, because he let out a low growl.

"I don't believe it," he muttered.

"What—" Then she shushed herself, blood flowing cold.

Dogs bayed in the distance, so faintly she could have imagined it, but she hadn't. Not when Hunter had heard the sound, too. Trembles seized her limbs as her mind blanked, and a whimper escaped her throat.

Hunter wrapped his solid arms around her. "Hang

in there." His words and warmth restored a measure of sanity. "I'm going to have to lay a false trail while you wait here with bitty boy. They're miles behind us. You'll be fine until I get back. Then we'll have to walk in the water upstream for a while to give the dogs the best chance of following the false scent."

"You're leaving me?" Blackness, not from the night, closed in around her.

"I'm trusting you." He guided her to a deadfall tree trunk a short way from the stream, shrugged out of his pack and laid it on the ground. With deft movements, he detached the rifle. "Should I leave this with you? Do you know how to use it?"

Mouth dry as dust, mind scurrying like a rat in a maze, Karissa barely managed to shake her head. "Never used one," she mumbled. "I'd be pretty useless with it."

"I'll take it then." Hunter slung the rifle across his back. "There's trail mix in the pack and bottled water. Take the opportunity to fortify yourself."

Nodding wordlessly, she plopped onto the natural forest bench. Her feet and legs instantly relished the relief, but the distant baying of the dogs turned her insides to quivering mush. How long did they have until slavering jaws closed in?

Stop it!

Indulging such mental images was counterproductive. She inhaled a deep breath and released it in ragged puffs. He said he was trusting her. Somehow those were the right words, the exact encouragement she needed. Her spine straightened, and she looked up at Hunter.

"*Vaya con Dios*, or go with God, as some of my Belizean friends would say. Kyle and I will be right here when you get back."

"I know you will." He brushed his fingers across her cheek, leaving a trail of tingling fire against her skin. Then he was gone, splashing across the stream and vanishing into the dark tree cover.

Karissa snuggled the sleeping baby close, more for her sake than his. Hunter had been right about the chill in the forest after dark. Now that she wasn't exerting herself, the coolness began to seep into her. But physical comfort was the least of her desires.

Answers.

She needed them, craved them. Who was so determined to kill her and why? Of course, the obvious answer was to shut her up about anything she might have seen at the murder site. Yet the effort to stamp her out seemed too relentless, too pointedly vicious for that explanation to satisfy. Why continue to expose himself by pursuing her with such elaborate ploys when he could simply have gone into hiding until time made it apparent whether or not she knew anything that could help the police? He could eliminate her later in a far less conspicuous fashion well before she could testify at trial. She'd read about such things happening.

But what if the truth went deeper? What if the reason was wrapped up in *why* Nikki was killed in the first place? What if her cousin hadn't been the only target— or maybe even the real target? The thought hit her like a punch in the gut, and the air left her lungs in a gush.

Following the shocking accident that claimed her parents' lives and then the tragic death of her twin sister, Karissa had gone ahead with her plans to leave for

Belize. She'd thought the change of scenery would deliver her from the paranoia she'd begun to feel in the States that someone was out to get her family. Now she had to ask herself if her earlier fears were well founded. After all, just because a person thought someone was out to get them didn't mean they were mentally unstable. Sometimes it was true. But who could possibly hate the Landon family so much?

Hunter trotted through the woods, deliberately swiping his hands across tree trunks. Every now and then he stopped and rolled in the compost of the forest floor. The extra-strong scent would keep the dogs interested. Then he'd get up and run again, teeth gritted, heart hammering like a piston.

A furnace blazed in the core of his belly that hadn't been stoked to this degree since that childhood day he'd dealt with a gang of bullies that came after his little brother on the playground. Then, he'd shocked himself—not to mention his parents, who'd been called in to sort out the aftermath—as well as Jace, who'd been in stunned awe of the black eyes his usually mild-mannered brother had delivered. After that, no one had wanted to get on his bad side or mess with his kid brother. And the criteria for his adult career had been set—something that tapped into the protective instincts embedded in his genes. Firefighter had fit that bill until he'd plowed headfirst into a wall of his human frailty.

At this moment, rather than attempting to subtly mislead a pack of hounds and whoever followed them, everything in him strained to go on the offensive against the ruthless killer who was targeting a woman without any regard for the baby in her care. Hunter's hands balled into fists. His priority had to be getting Karissa and the child to safety, but after that he was going to have a hard time stepping back and letting law enforcement handle everything—especially if the perpetrator was still determined to snuff out the woman and child's lives. He simply wasn't wired to ignore threats—especially threats to someone vulnerable.

After a long mile of laying scent, Hunter turned back. His insides itched to verify the safety of his charges. What if he'd underestimated the amount of time their pursuers would need to catch up with them? He swatted the self-defeating thought away. The baying of the hounds still sounded sporadically but not yet close enough to create urgency. He had to believe he and Karissa would have time to implement the second half of his plan.

Soon, the thin mewl of a fussing infant met his ears. Kyle had awakened—probably hungry. Abruptly, the crying stopped, and Hunter's heart did a wild jump in his chest. Had something happened to silence the child? Electricity surged through his legs, sending him at reckless speed back over ground he'd recently covered. The tinkle of water flowing over rocks met his ears, and he slowed, pulling the rifle off his back and holding it ready. He crept forward carefully so as not to charge into an ambush. Scarcely daring to breathe, he halted at the tree line and examined the far bank of the cold stream that originated somewhere high in the mountains where snow was perpetual.

The outline of a petite figure perched on the log where he'd left her, but what was she doing? She seemed to be reaching out, touching something, and then returning her hand to her chest—no, to the baby in the sling in front of her.

"Karissa," he called softly as he lowered the rifle.

Her head came up, but he couldn't make out her features.

"You're back." Relief weighted her voice.

Hunter splashed across the stream and joined her at the fallen log. In one hand, she held a handkerchief that had come out of the pack. Next to her sat the small plastic storage container that used to hold trail mix. Now it hosted something liquid.

The baby let out a noise like a cross between a snarl and a sneeze then started to fuss again. Karissa bounced him in his sling, making shushing noises, as she reached over and dipped the corner of the hankie in the liquid and then brought it to the infant's mouth. The little guy sucked noisily.

Karissa let out a soft laugh. "Kyle woke up mad as a hornet that his belly was empty. I'm sorry but feeding him took priority over preserving the trail mix." With her foot, she nudged the pile of seeds, nuts and dried oats and fruit that had been dumped on the ground. "His bottle and formula were incinerated with the cabin, so I'm improvising with powdered milk I found in the pack and mixed with water. He may get a bellyache from it, or he may not, but at least it will quiet him for a while. Your trail diversion won't work well if a bawling baby leads our pursuers right to us."

Hunter drew in a deep breath and let it out in a chuckle. "Just when I think you can't amaze me further, you do it again. How long do you think it will take for him to be satisfied? We have no time to waste."

"I have no idea. Can you give us five minutes or so?"

"Okay," he answered. Not that he was actually sure it would be okay or not.

Too wound up to sit beside Karissa on the log, Hunter donned his pack and moved deeper into the trees back in the direction they'd come from. Those dogs, and presumably their armed handlers, were closing in. He might not be able to allow her a full five minutes.

Two minutes dragged past, and the hairs on the back of Hunter's neck were standing on end from the hungry bay of the nearing pack. Hunter hurried to the log to find Karissa standing up and adjusting the sling.

"I'm ready," she said. "He fell asleep again in mid-suck, and hopefully he will stay asleep for a while." The strain in her tone let him know that she was all too aware of the hounds closing in.

He nodded and led the way into water that, at this time of the summer, came only up to his ankles. She followed without a word of protest, though the chill of the mountain stream must be nipping her skin through those canvas sneakers. He hardly felt the cold through his hiking boots. Sticking close to her, he lent support by grabbing her elbow any time she seemed to totter on the slick rocks at the bottom of the stream. Soon, whenever he took her arm, her shivers were obvious. Still, she did not complain, even when the water deepened to his calves, and he also started getting a taste of the cold. She must be freezing like an icicle.

His respect for this petite dynamo climbed another several notches. Unfortunately, they were going to have to remain in the water for a considerable distance in order for the ploy to have any chance of working. The baying of the pack drew close—much closer than Hunter liked. He practically held his breath, straining to know if the dogs would follow the false trail or pick up their true scent.

Karissa leaned close into him, her shivers pronounced. "If they find us now," she murmured, "I won't be able to run. If that happens, I want you to take the baby and get him to safety."

Everything in Hunter begged to cry out, *Forget it. We stand or fall together.*

"We'll see if that time comes," he said instead. Sure, bitty boy had to be the priority, but if their enemies closed in, he had his rifle and would use it first before fleeing as the last resort.

Hunter pulled them to a halt, the better to listen. The dogs were coming. Their ravening tones echoed between the trees. Then the baying suddenly ceased. Hunter imagined the pack sniffing the area near the log where they had stopped and then vacated, and then splashing back and forth across the stream. In his mind's eye, he pictured them milling and sniffing, noses to the ground, trying to determine the direction their prey had fled. Would they fall for the deception?

All at once, a single hound let out a howl then the others joined in. The bedlam sounded too close, almost on top of them. The animals hadn't fallen for the deception. Hunter's gut wound tight, and he started to reach for his rifle.

No...wait! He stood absolutely still, holding his breath.

Seconds ticked past, and little by little, the baying began to fade. Hunter allowed himself to breathe again just as Karissa collapsed against him. He caught her up and, cradling her in his arms, made his way out of the stream. Moving as quickly as he could with his precious cargo, Hunter reset his trajectory by the stars and headed for their eventual destination. He couldn't imagine a safer place to take his charges. But then, he'd imagined himself safe from almost anything at his cabin retreat, and look how that had turned out.

"Hunter?" Karissa's small voice drove his negative thoughts away.

He looked down to find her gazing up at him with a bemused twist to her lips.

"So much for my scoffing at the idea of you carrying me," she said with a thin laugh. "You can put me down now. I can wiggle my toes again."

"Don't push yourself," he answered. "I'm doing fine. You don't weigh much more than a feather." What was the matter with him that he didn't want to let go of her?

She swatted him on the arm. "I know better than that. Put...me...down."

He sighed and halted. "Whatever you say, milady." Gently, he set her on her feet but kept an arm around her shoulder as she got her bearings. "Doing okay?"

"I think so." She took a step out of his grasp and gave a nod. "More feeling will return as we get moving."

"Glad you're of the mind-set to keep on our way. We won't be able to stop anymore. If our hunters are persistent, they'll backtrack when the scent runs out, and the dogs could pick up the right trail again eventually as they range up and down the stream. Depends on how long their handlers will let them sniff around. I want us out of their reach before they can catch up."

"Lead on." She motioned him forward.

The rest of the night passed with no hint of dogs on their trail. Yet Hunter couldn't shake a sense of unease. As the sky lightened toward dawn, they reached the abandoned logging road. It wasn't much more than a rain-rutted dirt track anymore. Hunter kept them on the edge of it, partially under cover of the trees as they negotiated a downward path. Karissa said not a word, her breathing coming in strong huffs and occasional puffs.

"Can I take bitty boy for you?" he asked.

"He's still asleep, so let's not disturb him," she answered.

Hunter led on. Not long later, with the sun almost fully above the horizon, the back of a squat, clapboard building loomed in their path at the bottom of a steep incline.

"Wait here." He turned and directed Karissa to a seat on a nearby stump.

"I thought you said these people were friendly."

"They are, but we have no idea if they've been visited by whoever is looking for us. A remote possibility, but considering the resources of who we're dealing with, I don't care to take chances. If the coast is clear, I'll be right back for you. If not and I don't return or you hear some kind of ruckus, head straight west and you'll come to a ranger station—hopefully manned by a real ranger."

They exchanged grimaces as Karissa brushed a thick hank of hair back from her face. A determined smile lifted the corners of her mouth, but her eyes betrayed deep weariness. Still, despite the hardships of the night, she radiated a winsome purity and strength that drew on Hunter's heart.

God, help me to be here for this woman and child every second until we get this matter resolved. And somehow please keep the truth about my identity from her until that happens.

"I'll be right here." She gazed up at him with enormous eyes. "You'll be back."

"Hold that thought." He turned and began negotiating his step-sliding way down the dirt incline.

"I'll be praying."

Her simple pledge bathed him in warmth and accelerated his pace. He reached the back of the bar and sidled up against the side of the building as he peered around the corner. Even this early in the morning, the portion of the parking lot in his view held a few motorcycles—several Harleys and a vintage Indian, all belonging to regulars that he knew. Likely the bikes had been there overnight, since a back room contained numerous bunks, and a lot of the gang virtually lived here.

The Indian belonged to Hunter's friend and the owner of the place, Thomas Buckley III. Hunter still had a hard time wrapping his mind around the fact that his Christian biker buddy had been born with a silver spoon in his mouth, lost the family spoon to Daddy's bad investments, devolved into an embittered member of the infamous Outlaws motorcycle gang, wound up in prison and then transformed into a follower of Christ. Most folks simply knew the guy as Buck with nothing but guesses as to his background. Something about Hunter's quiet suffering had drawn Thomas's full testimony from him one rainy day as they sat across from each other in a booth sipping hot java and shooting the breeze. The tattooed biker's trust in him and freely given spiritual mentorship had done a lot for Hunter when he was in a very low place.

Hunter glanced back the way he had come. Was that a portion of Karissa's sneaker barely poking out from her cover position? Wise woman. She was staying still, and hopefully the baby would remain asleep until his recognizance was completed.

Ducking slightly for no good reason except his mindfulness of stealth, Hunter slid along one side of the building toward the front. As more of the parking lot came into view, revealing no additional vehicles, he exhaled a long breath. No one here except bikers—unless someone had walked in from the distant highway. Not likely.

Hunter rounded the corner and stepped up onto the low wooden porch. A wide window beckoned, offering a view inside. The large patron area was vacant, though a pool table sported balls in disarray across its top, the long bar held a cribbage board and cards, and a nearby booth featured an unfinished chess game. The normal gospel music with a country twang was not yet playing on the jukebox, but the strong odor of freshly ground coffee beans teased his nostrils. Someone here was awake.

A soft creak sounded on the boards behind Hunter. He began to whirl, but a prod in his back from something hard froze him in place.

"Lay that rifle down then put your hands up and turn around slow," growled an unfamiliar voice behind him.

Hunter complied and found himself gazing down the double barrels of a shotgun. At the other end of the gun stood a short, round man sporting a beard that put Hunter's to shame. The man glared at him with eyes the color of pine bark.

"State your business," he bit out.

"I'm here to see Buck."

"You know Buck? Then why are you sneaking around like a polecat?"

"I'll explain it to *him*. Since when did Buck station armed guards around the place?"

"Since we heard on the radio this morning about the woman murdered in the area. Another woman and a baby are missing. The police want to find her as a possible kidnapper, along with some former firefighter who's not right in the head. The dude called in a fake bomb threat to the Umpqua power project, torched a ranger cabin in the woods and went missing around the same time as the woman and kid. 'Course, Buck says the nutso firefighter didn't do anything bad, and we're to keep a lookout for strangers. You look like a stranger to me."

Hunter's gut clenched. The authorities thought Karissa and he were involved in a bomb threat, arson, kidnapping and murder? How did they come up with that idea? Of course, Karissa said she had left her purse and vehicle behind when she fled with Kyle. The authorities would have found those things and no baby in a home where there should have been one. The leap in logic wasn't great, and he couldn't deny the timing of the bomb threat and the arson on his cabin were also

suspicious, potentially tying him into the whole murder/
kidnapping scenario.

"I could call you a stranger, too. I've never met you,
and I've been here plenty of times."

"Came in a week ago. Bronto's my cousin," the man
said, naming one of the other members of the gang.
"Now, who are *you*?" A click sounded as he pulled back
the hammer on the shotgun.

Hunter faded his weight onto the balls of his feet in
preparation to leap aside, though he didn't stand much
chance of avoiding a load of buckshot at this range. "The
not-so-nutso ex-firefighter. I've had it with people coming after me with deadly weapons, so either pull that
trigger or take me to Buck."

"What's going on out here?" Buck's familiar voice
interrupted the face-off.

"Caught this guy sneaking around," said the guy
with the shotgun.

Buck lumbered up beside them. He was a big man,
beefy all over. A maze of multicolored tattoos ran up
and down his arms and around his thick neck, some
from his BC—before Christ—days and some from
after. A big one on his lower arm used to be a bloody
knife, but it had been transformed into an intricate and
poignant cross.

The forearm bearing the cross motioned toward the
gun. "Will you please put that thing down, Steggy, before you shoot off your big toe? This guy is a brother."

Hunter snorted a laugh. Bronto's nickname was short
for brontosaurus, because he was built like one, so for
his cousin that meant… "Steggy, as in stegosaurus?"

The hammer of the shotgun eased down, and the

weapon lowered. Steggy grinned, displaying crooked teeth. "That's me. You may be nuts, but you got guts." The man stuck out his hand, and Hunter shook it.

"Come in and give us the 411." Buck slapped Hunter on the shoulder. "Sounds like you're in a peck of trouble, but I know the news dudes and the cops got it wrong about who did what."

Hunter faced his friend and shook his head. "I can't come in yet. The missing woman and baby are with me, all right, but I'm protecting them, not kidnapping them. And she's not a killer or a kidnapper, either. They're waiting up in the forest. I came down to make sure none of these strangers Steggy was looking out for were hanging around."

Buck let out a low whistle. "Well, let's go fetch them."

With a nod, Hunter led them back the way he had come.

"This story just gets stranger and stranger," Steggy grumbled from the rear of the procession.

"You haven't heard the half of it yet," Hunter said.

They reached the base of the steep incline.

"All clear. We're coming up," he called to Karissa, and began the climb. He'd take the baby, and Buck and Steggy could help her down.

No answer came from the edge of the forest. No movement, either.

Hunter's heart leaped into his throat as he scrambled upward, tossing all caution to the wind. He and his companions arrived at the log where he'd left his charges. Kyle lay sleeping under the shelter of a nearby bush, still wrapped in his sling, but Karissa was nowhere to be seen.

FOUR

It happened so fast!

One moment Karissa was closing her eyes, succumbing to the exhaustion that wrapped her like a cloak, and the next her eyes popped wide as something cold and hard pressed into the back of her head.

"Don't cry out," a low, harsh voice said. "Where's the boyfriend?"

A strangled noise escaped Karissa's throat. How did she answer that? This was probably not the time to quibble about Hunter's non-boyfriend status. She simply lifted one hand and pointed to the bar below.

The man with the gun against her head grunted and grabbed her shoulder. "Too bad. It would have been better to scoop him up now as well. I will leave that to someone else. Put the baby down. You're coming with me."

Karissa complied quickly, ducking her head out of Kyle's sling and laying him tenderly in a patch of soft grass under the protective boughs of a bush. If she was falling into the hands of a killer, there was no way she wanted Kyle with her.

Then she was yanked around and shoved into the woods, her captor following close behind. He began pushing her at an uncomfortable pace. Every beat of her thundering heart racked her body, and every sense seemed magnified a hundred times. Piney and loamy odors assailed her nostrils, and her breath caught at each snap of a dry twig beneath her feet. She hadn't yet glimpsed the person holding the gun and directing her progress with muttered curses and prods with the barrel of his firearm.

"The boss can just sue me," the thug mumbled under his breath as he shoved her along.

"Sue you for what?"

"Not grabbing the kid. I don't mess with kids, you know. I've got standards."

"But you tried to burn us all up in that cabin."

"I didn't give that order. Not my doing."

"But someone shot at me at Nikki's cabin while I was carrying the baby. Was that you?"

"How was I to know you had the kid with you?"

Karissa's mouth gaped open. Amazing how self-righteous a hired gunman could make himself sound and believe every word of his own blather.

"Clearly, you have no such standards when it comes to me," she said. "Why didn't you just shoot me and leave me there on the road?" She bit her lower lip. If only she could recall the heedless question before it popped out of her mouth.

"Shut up and move faster!"

The gun barrel jabbed into her back again, and she winced. She was going to have a cluster of round bruises…if she lived long enough to develop them.

Karissa scurried down a short slope, stumbled on a tree root and pitched forward. A hand clasped her elbow and stopped her from face-planting on the ground. She righted herself and looked toward the man who now stood beside her still squeezing her elbow in a vise grip. Her gaze first met the black hole of his gun then traveled up the barrel to take in his navy blue shirt then a leathery neck and a beaky nose, and finally to lock stares with flat brown eyes beneath a mop of dark hair. Yes, this was the man who'd shot at her at her cousin's house. Almost certainly the one who'd killed Nikki.

"Why did you leave my cousin's place after killing her and then come back again?" When would her mouth learn to stop speaking before thinking?

Her captor grinned, stretching a white slash of a scar that marred his upper lip. "No cell reception. I needed to make a call, and I'd already disabled the lady's landline before I went in after her. You weren't supposed to show up yet."

His dead eyes studied her—like being under the scrutiny of an alligator or a shark. Karissa swallowed against a dry throat. Apparently, the assassin didn't care if she saw his face. As if she needed any confirmation that she was marked for death.

"If I had my way, I would have dropped you back there or right here and now," the man grated out. "But since we didn't catch you last night and the authorities are swarming, the boss says we need to stage the scene carefully to confirm their suspicions that you killed your cousin and snatched the baby with the help of that firefighter."

Karissa's jaw sagged. The police thought she'd

killed Nikki and kidnapped Kyle? And that Hunter had helped? Of course, the authorities would have all her information from her abandoned purse and car. Hopefully, they were also asking themselves what sort of kidnapper left that stuff behind.

Her captor's lips twisted into a nasty smile. "Nice of you to leave us your handbag containing the car keys so we could grab the vehicle but leave some incriminating belongings of yours in the house."

Her gut clenched. So much for the presence of the purse and car creating doubt in the authorities' minds. She had to assume the perpetrators were instead going to use those things to create some of that staging this guy had mentioned.

"Hunter knows I didn't kidnap Kyle or kill anyone, because you goons showed up and tried to kill *us*."

"No worries." The man shrugged. "Some of the other guys are on the way and will take out the firefighter and anyone else you've managed to involve. The boss will lay those killings at your doorstep, too. Now keep moving."

A deep chill settled in Karissa's core as they trekked onward. So, there was indeed a mysterious boss behind the horrendous attack on her cousin and now her and even Hunter because of his involvement with her. But who could he or she be, and what could be the motive? Whatever was going on was despicable, especially when an infant was deprived of his mother and could easily have been hurt in all that had transpired so far. Now Kyle was abandoned on the edge of the woods all alone. Hopefully, Hunter would soon find him, but what might happen to Hunter and the baby when her captor's threatened reinforcements arrived didn't bear thinking about. Embers of heat began to displace the chill in her gut.

All at once, Karissa's stomach growled, and the man chuckled. She gritted her teeth against angry words. How charming that he found her hunger and discomfort amusing. Not that she really had any interest in a last meal before this creep and his mystery boss carried out their plans for her.

Not long later, they climbed a berm onto a narrow gravel road where a black pickup sat idling. It was the truck the gunman at her back had driven up to Nikki's house only yesterday. Karissa's captor shoved her into the back seat and climbed in beside her, gun still pointed in her direction. The blond man behind the wheel took off in a spurt of gravel.

Hunter raced through the forest with Buck on his heels. Steggy had been sent back to deliver the baby to Buck's wife, where he would receive good care. Karissa and her abductor had left a fairly obvious trail of trampled grass and weeds and snapped twigs, so they were likely relying on speed rather than cunning to elude any pursuit. They couldn't be far ahead, yet he hadn't caught a glimpse of them. If only there hadn't been that delay on the bar's porch while Steggy interrogated him. Worse, Hunter had left his rifle where he'd set it down when Steggy ordered him to do so. Hunter leaped over a fallen branch and plunged down a shallow draw then up again, lungs sucking in deep drafts of piney air and blood pumping as fast as his feet.

What if the captor got away with Karissa before they could catch up? No, he couldn't think like that. At least, they'd found no evidence that the kidnapper had killed her yet. Speculating as to why not was futile. He could only be thankful. If the abductor's trajectory continued in this direction, they were likely headed for a nearby service road. A picture of a coal-black pickup truck flashed before his mind's eye, the vehicle that had carried destruction to the ranger cabin and nearly to themselves.

How had the murderer found them? Another futile question with insufficient data to provide an answer. Hunter mentally kicked himself. He'd been so sure they'd lost their pursuers because they'd heard no dogs. He'd been wrong and had left his charges vulnerable and alone.

The slam of a vehicle door taunted his ears. The sound had to be from the kidnapper's vehicle waiting to carry Karissa to whatever doom was planned.

Hunter plunged up the bank leading to the service road. He burst from the tree line to spot the black truck that had carried men with weapons to his cabin yesterday. Hunter scurried up behind it, ducking to keep from being spotted in the driver's mirror. He had barely wrapping his hands around the top of the tailgate, keeping his head down below it, when the vehicle spun its tires and accelerated in a burst of flying dust and gravel, dragging him with it.

Karissa struggled with her seat belt.

"Why bother?" The man with the gun chuckled.

The blond man echoed the chuckle. "Why not? We want to deliver her safe and sound to Portland."

Karissa ignored them as she clicked the belt home.

She turned her face toward the pine forest whizzing past. Where was Hunter? Was he coming after her? She couldn't imagine him reacting any other way to her disappearance. He must be frantic. But what possibility did he have of finding her now that she was being whisked away in a vehicle? Slim to none. And even if he did catch up with her, he'd almost certainly end up dead along with her.

No, her only hope was God, always had been, always would be. She'd keep her eyes open...waiting...ready to grab the slightest opportunity.

Hunter hiked his feet up onto the bumper but continued to hunker down behind the tailgate, hoping against hope that his clinging fingers were not noticed by Karissa's captors. He couldn't hang on in this awkward position forever. Besides, they would come to a paved road shortly, and any traffic behind them would notice him and likely honk or in some way signal the driver that they had a weird extra passenger. He needed to make his move before that happened, while he still had the element of surprise. What he needed was a distraction.

Cautiously, he let go of the tailgate with one hand and dug around in his jeans pocket. His fingers closed around the handle of his multitool Swiss army knife. It was a bit of a trick to wriggle it out of his pocket in his crouched position, but he finally managed it. The fingers of his clinging hand were starting to cramp, but he ordered them to hang on a little longer as the vehicle jounced and bumped along the lightly maintained road.

Muscles screaming for relief, Hunter edged to the corner of the bumper. Then he flipped open his knife and reached around the side, jabbing toward the passenger-side rear tire. *Please, God, don't let anyone in the front seat be looking in the side-view mirror.* The knife sank into the tire, but the whirling motion ripped the weapon from Hunter's hand. The vehicle lurched; he lost his grip on the tailgate and went flying. Flipping in midair, Hunter landed splat on his back in the ditch. Every molecule of wind left his lungs, and his vision blacked out. Forever seconds later, the forest swam into view once more, and he drew precious oxygen into his chest.

Where was the truck?

Hunter lay still and listened. Tires skidded on gravel then halted, abruptly followed by a door opening, and a harsh voice inflaming the air with curses.

A second door opened. "You idiot! Don't tell me you didn't check the tires before we left on this assignment."

"What did you call me?" the first voice snarled back.

A third door opened. "I believe your friend thinks you were stupid and negligent," Karissa said.

Good girl. Keep them riled with each other.

Hunter grinned as he rolled over onto his stomach and began crawling toward the pickup. The bank was steep here, so he was out of sight for the moment, and the men's ongoing argument provided a degree of cover for any sound he was making. It was still going to be a major trick to overpower two armed men and free their captive without someone getting hurt. If he had to take a bullet, he'd be okay with that, but not with the death or injury of an innocent woman.

Hunter's hand fell on something hard and metallic. He looked down. His knife. It must have been flung by centrifugal force from the shredded tire and landed in the ditch the same way he had. *Thank You, God.* He was literally bringing a knife to a gunfight, but he'd take what he could get.

Knife in his fist, he scooted upward to the lip of the berm and peered onto the road. A tall blond man was struggling to retrieve the spare tire and jack from under the truck box. His back was to Hunter. A stocky, scar-lipped man was glaring at his partner while holding his gun trained on Karissa, who stood beside the open rear pickup door.

"You better make this fast," said Scar Lip to Blondie. "No telling if the boyfriend is already on our trail. At the very least, he's probably called the cops to tell his side of the story and get them looking for us, which is a complication the boss is *not* going to like. We were supposed to get our hands on *him*, too, before he could talk to anyone."

"Yeah, well, the boss has cops in his pocket all over this state, so stop sweating. And if you don't like the way I'm changing this tire—" the tall man grunted as he hefted the spare onto the ground "—you can do it yourself."

Muttering something under his breath, Scar Lip whirled toward Karissa, presenting his back to Hunter. "Get in the truck and stay there," he snarled at his captive.

Pale-faced, Karissa began to comply.

Hunter's opportunity wasn't going to get any better, but he needed the gun trained away from Karissa. He snatched up a rock and tossed it into the bushes several feet up the road. Scar Lip turned and froze, gun pointed in the direction of the noise. Hunter stood and threw the knife at the gunman. The blade flew true, thanks to lots of practice while he entertained himself alone at the cabin, and buried itself in the bicep of the man's gun arm. The pistol discharged even as he dropped it, though the silencer kept the sound to a low pop. However, the shriek the man let out startled birds into squawking and flapping from the trees overhead.

Rushing forward, Hunter didn't waste time on the man screaming and pawing for the knife buried in the back of his arm. In midstride, Hunter swooped up the tire iron lying on the ground near the spare. Even as the blond man, eyes wide and mouth agape, reached for the gun in his shoulder holster, Hunter brought the iron down on his head. The man dropped like a stone and lay still.

Hunter whirled for the other man he'd injured with the knife to find him using his left hand to claw out a small pistol from his waistband. Teeth bared, the man trained the little gun, deadly at this range, straight into Hunter's face. His heart squeezed in on itself. He'd tried and failed to save Karissa.

The rear passenger door sprang open and struck the gunman even as the man fired. The bullet went wild, and Hunter swung the tire iron, dropping a second kidnapper into the dust.

He rushed for Karissa, and she fell sobbing out of the back seat into his arms.

FIVE

Karissa sat at a table in the coffee bean–smelling biker bar, sipping hot tea and working on a plate of scrambled eggs with toast and jam on the side. Every few seconds a small shudder rippled through her—residual effects of recent terror. Nearby, Kyle chortled as Buck's plump, pretty wife Starla and several of the other biker women showered him with attention. Amazingly, diapers and formula had been on hand at the bar, and Kyle was changed, fed and reveling in adoration.

Buck said his gang always had baby stuff available to hand out when they did outreaches in struggling neighborhoods. Despite his rough outward appearance, he was clearly well educated. He had caught up with them on the service road soon after Hunter had made short work of her captors. Now the two gunmen were tied up and stashed under guard in a storage shed, awaiting the arrival of the county sheriff.

A hand fell on Karissa's shoulder, and she nearly jumped out of her skin.

"Sorry for startling you." Hunter backed off with his hands raised.

She sent him a wry smile. "No, I'm sorry for being so edgy."

"With good reason. A whole lot has happened in less than twenty-four hours. The sheriff will be here soon. Once those jokers out in the storage shed tell him who their boss is, it'll all be over."

Karissa motioned for Hunter to sit down beside her.

She leaned toward him. "I'm a little worried about that." Her words emerged in a near whisper.

"You don't think those guys will talk?" His low tones matched hers.

"Sure, there's that, and the fact that the authorities are going to have to believe our story and revise their opinion about our involvement in Nikki's death, as well as Kyle's removal from his mother's house."

"I'm fairly easy on that score, since we have those two hired goons and Buck as a witness that we're telling the truth about them snatching you. It's not going to be a great leap for them to shift the blame for everything onto them."

"I hope you're right, but the scar-lipped one—the one who killed Nikki—said there were others like him coming here to finish you off and anyone with you. Also, the blond guy said their boss has law enforcement 'all over the state'—" she bracketed those last few words in air quotation marks "—on his payroll."

Hunter leaned back in his chair and let out a whistle under his breath. "As to the former, the folks here have hearts of gold, but if we're attacked, they're tougher than nails. Any gang of those thugs' henchmen will have a rotten time of it. As to the latter, then for sure

I'm not letting you and bitty boy out of my sight until I know you're in trustworthy hands."

Karissa cocked her head at her rescuer and protector. "You're not responsible for me, you know. I got you into a mess that has nothing to do with you."

"Uh-uh!" Hunter shook his head emphatically. "None of this is your fault, including my involvement. The fault is entirely on your attackers. They chose to do what they're doing."

"But why?" Karissa's exclamatory question burst out loud and shrill.

Conversations and activity in the bar stilled as eyes focused on her and Hunter.

Karissa's cheeks heated. "Sorry, everyone. I'm a little upset."

Starla, smiled at her over Kyle's downy head as she cuddled him. "You're asking the right question, honey, and I'd say you're braver than most. Hang in there."

Karissa hauled in a long breath and let it out slowly. She stood up and looked around the room populated with men and women sporting leather and chains, some with scraggly beards or wild hair, and almost all with a myriad of tats decorating their skin.

Her heart filled with warmth. "Thank you so much, every one of you. I will never forget your kindness in helping us out."

Choruses of "it was nothing" or "no problem" answered her, and rugged faces beamed at her.

Buck sauntered over. "Hunter here is a good dude to have on your side. God's working out a plan in you meeting up."

Something significant passed between the two men

in their gazes toward one another. Hunter's stare fell away, and he shifted from foot to foot. Buck just smiled benignly. Karissa's brows snapped together. What was that all about? The biker wouldn't be trying to play matchmaker, would he? This was hardly the time or the place, regardless of the attraction she did indeed feel for the brave man who'd been risking his life for her. But what else could the issue be that would have Hunter acting like a cat on a hot tin roof?

The sound of tires on gravel drew attention toward the door. The whole room seemed to hold its breath.

"It's the sheriff and a deputy in two separate cars," Steggy called out from his lookout station at one of the windows.

A measure of tension leached out of Karissa's shoulders. Not some sort of attack then. Time alone would tell if the law enforcement representatives were trustworthy or not. She exchanged a long, steady look with Hunter.

Then her attention was drawn toward the front of the building as heavy footfalls sounded on the porch boards. The door opened to admit a sturdily-built woman and a thin man, both in sheriff's office uniforms.

"Peg O'Rourke, Douglas County sheriff," said the woman in the lead. "What have you got for me?"

Buck stepped forward and explained the situation in terse words. However, focus quickly fastened on Karissa and Hunter, and Karissa soon found herself seated at a table across from the sheriff, telling her story, while Hunter sat with the deputy.

"I only want the basics right now," Sheriff O'Rourke reminded her when Karissa started to go off on a rabbit trail in her explanation. "We'll get detailed statements at the station." The blue-eyed woman paused in her note-taking and smiled at her.

Karissa offered a tentative smile back. The sheriff seemed both businesslike and kind. It was hard to imagine her on any crook's payroll. Maybe everything was going to be okay now. The fist around her heart loosened its grip a slight degree.

"There was no sign of a break-in at Nikki's place." Karissa tagged the information onto the back of her story. "The front door was unlocked, actually. That's how I got in. Somehow, that guy we have out in the shed tricked her into inviting him in. I don't know if that detail offers any leads or not, but it's what I observed."

"A valid deduction that I'm sure the investigators will take into account." The sheriff nodded and stood up. "Okay, then," she addressed the room in general. "We'll collect the prisoners now and take Ms. Landon and Mr. Raines with us. There will still be many questions they will have to answer, not just to my office, but the Oregon State Police. Buck—" she stabbed her pencil in the biker's direction "—you and whoever else was directly involved in this mess need to come on in and give a statement as soon as possible also."

"Me and Steggy will follow you on into Roseburg." Buck nodded toward the sheriff then winked at Karissa.

"I'll ride in the car with Kyle and Karissa," Hunter stated in a tone that defied argument.

A genuine smile dawned on Karissa's face. How could anything go wrong with protectors like these? Then she sobered.

"Sheriff O'Rourke, Kyle's so comfortable here, and it sounds like Hunter and I are going to be very busy answering questions for a while. Maybe we should leave him in these good people's care for the time being."

A pang gripped her at the thought of not having Kyle close by. Strange how the little guy had so quickly wormed his way into her heart but leaving him for his safety was for the best when people were after her to do her harm.

"No problem," Buck said.

Starla grinned, and the other women nodded with happy smiles—some of the guys, too. Clearly, Kyle was busy stealing other people's hearts, too, not just hers.

"We'll give him a bath and change his clothes," Starla said.

"I think we've even got a baby swing and a playpen around here somewhere," Buck added.

"Don't tell me." Karissa laughed. "You give those away on your outreaches, too."

Buck shrugged. "Guilty as charged."

Then his mouth fell ajar, and his gaze flew toward the sheriff at his slip into terminology anyone would hesitate to use around law enforcement, not to mention an ex-con. The whole room erupted into laughter as Buck's cheeks reddened. The sheriff and the deputy chuckled with the rest of them, and Buck joined in. The guy was a good sport.

Soon Hunter was seated next to the deputy in the man's car, while Karissa had the back all to herself. Out ahead was the sheriff with the two battered gunmen in her back seat. The rumble of a pair of motorcycles carried to Karissa's ears from Buck and Steggy in the rear of the procession. For the first time in many hours, Karissa felt completely safe. Her head lolled against the seatback, and she closed her eyes.

A horrendous crash catapulted her awake. Pain engulfed her right side, and her head snapped sideways, slamming against a solid barrier—the passenger-side window. She saw stars as her body rammed against her seat belt to the tune of the *pop-pop* of the front airbags exploding.

Hunter swallowed a spate of chalk dust from the airbag and his lungs spasmed with the effort of coughing. The dust clouded his vision, and his chest ached like he'd been smacked by a rogue fire hose that had escaped its handlers' grips.

What had happened?

He forced his aching neck to turn. The deputy was slumped against the steering wheel, limp and eyes closed. He appeared to be breathing, though. The glass from the shattered side window littered the man's back. Hunter turned farther to find Karissa rubbing the side of her head. Her fingers came away red from a gash in her scalp, and her gaze was cloudy and unfocused.

Karissa and the deputy's side of the vehicle was crumpled inward and some sort of massive SUV had its nose buried in the sheriff's department car, which canted into the ditch at a slant. With the force of that ramming job from the SUV, it was amazing the smaller vehicle hadn't flipped end over end. Their convoy had been moments from leaving the back roads and joining Highway 138 when this attack came. Where was the sheriff's car with the kidnappers inside? No sign of it. Where were Buck and Steggy? No sign of the motorcycles coming up behind, either. Hunter's heart shriveled. They were all alone against whatever manpower and firepower that SUV held.

These must be the reinforcements that Scar Lip had told Karissa about, and they would be climbing out of their vehicle momentarily and closing in on their prey. Hunter grabbed the deputy's Glock 22 sidearm and chambered a bullet. The deputy was in no shape to defend them, so it was up to him. He needed to direct any gunfire away from Karissa and the deputy and toward himself.

Hunter opened his door and rolled out onto the grassy berm. Nettles pricked his body through his thin shirt, but he paid no attention. The SUV's rear doors started to open, and Hunter sent three wild shots in the direction of the men starting to pile out of the ramming vehicle, intent on finishing what they had started. Hunter's gunshots had the desired effect, and the men retreated, SUV doors slamming closed. Hunter raced for the tree line. The big vehicle's engine revved as it backed away from the crumpled car and drove toward him broadside on the road. Windows came down and gun muzzles pointed toward Hunter as he reached tree cover. Automatic fire raked the trees.

Too bad he didn't at least have his rifle. The sheriff had put it in the trunk of her car, which had seemed logical at the time, but now potentially carried a more sinister explanation. She had ensured they were weaponless, probably not figuring on him grabbing the deputy's gun, and then she abandoned them.

Only twelve bullets remained in the Glock. He'd have to make them count. He peeked around his sheltering tree trunk and sent three more rounds into the SUV. A yelp rewarded him, but another rake of bullets also. They whizzed around him, shredding leaves and small branches that fell over him in a shower.

On the plus side, the shooters had their attention focused on him, just as he'd hoped, and Karissa was now sneaking out the rear passenger door, which was more than he'd hoped for in her dazed and probably concussed condition. However, instead of running for cover herself, she pulled open the front passenger side door and reached inside to tug at the sheriff's deputy in the driver's seat. The woman was remarkable. Apparently, the deputy was coming around, because he seemed to be helping her extricate him from the vehicle. Then the two of them tottered off, supporting one another, toward the cover of the forest.

Time to give their attackers more reason to keep their eyes on him, not the former occupants of the sheriff's department vehicle. Hunter darted to another tree, peered around and sent four more bullets toward the SUV. The answering *rat-a-tat-tat* flung him to the spongy undergrowth with fire spreading through his left bicep.

He was hit!

But Karissa and the deputy had reached the tree line. Now it was all between him and the goons in the SUV.

Hunter struggled to his feet, left arm useless. Warm wetness spread down it, but the blood wasn't spurting, so at least the brachial artery hadn't been hit, and he didn't think the bone was broken, either. He looked at the Glock clutched in his fist and pressed his lips into a grim line. Five bullets left and then…

Lord, I expect I'll be seeing You face-to-face soon. Please protect Karissa. Get her to safety and bring the guilty to justice. Amen!

Hunter blanked his mind against the pain in his arm, swung out of cover and slammed another pair of bullets toward the SUV's open windows. More yelping and cursing answered him as he darted to fresh cover, a spate of gunfire on his heels. A wave of dizziness passed through Hunter, and he leaned his weight against the white oak tree between him and the gunmen.

The sound of vehicle doors opening alerted him that the attackers were getting out of the SUV. He glanced around the tree trunk. They'd emerged on the side of the vehicle away from him. Made sense for them, but too bad for him because he couldn't pick them off... Or could he?

Hunter lowered himself to the ground. Yup. There they were. At least five sets of feet and trouser-clad lower legs showed beneath the SUV's undercarriage. Time to be a marksman. He took careful aim and fired at one of the exposed ankles. Someone shrieked and hit the ground. Hunter didn't wait to congratulate himself but took aim again and fired. Same result.

One bullet left and they knew it. The three still on their feet came for him, swarming around the vehicle, automatics blazing. Hunter rolled away from the line of fire, injured arm screaming protests. He came to rest at the base of a maple tree and gathered himself to expend his final bullet and take at least one more of these guys out of the equation.

The sudden distinctive blast of a shotgun froze Hunter's finger on the trigger. One of the gunmen crumpled, yelping and clutching his knee. The cavalry had come. The shotgun roared again, downing another attacker into a similar knee-clutching position. Gunman number three turned tail and ran back toward the SUV, but Hunter put his final bullet into the man's shoulder. The man fell and dropped his gun, clutching his wound and snarling curses.

Buck and Steggy emerged from the trees, the latter busily reloading his shotgun. Buck quickly rounded up the weapons from the five attackers. Then he joined Hunter, who was sitting with his back up against the trunk of the maple, hand clamped over his wound, attempting to stem the bleeding. Steggy got busy tying up the gunmen while Buck hunkered at Hunter's side and tightly bound up his arm with a handkerchief.

"Great to see you," Hunter said to his friend through gritted teeth. "What happened to you?" The bearded biker was covered in dirt and bloody scrapes.

Buck scowled. "Someone clotheslined us about a mile back. Strung a rope across the road right where we came around a curve. The ploy should have killed us, but whoever set it up miscalculated the height, and the clothesline just sent us top over tail. Our bikes are toast, but Steggy's shotgun was in its case and weathered the accident intact. So, he grabbed it and we had to hoof it to catch up with you."

Hunter grinned through his pain. Foot travel was a biker's most dreaded mode of transportation.

"Glad you finally made it to the party." Using the tree for support, Hunter struggled to his feet.

"You'd better sit down before you fall down," his friend said.

"Not happening. We need to find Karissa and the sheriff's deputy. I'm not sure what shape either of them is in, but they hightailed it into the woods when the shooting started."

"I suppose it's a waste of breath for me to advise you that Steggy and I can find them while you take it easy."

"You suppose correctly."

Buck grunted and turned toward Steggy, who had just joined them. "Stay here with our ambushers while Hunter and I look for our fleeing friends."

"And call this in to the state police," Hunter added. "Clearly, the sheriff's department is compromised. Someone from that office had to tell these goons what route we were taking and how our convoy was configured in getting to the station."

"Gotcha." Steggy offered them a two-fingered salute to the forehead and trotted away.

"Hand me one of those gunny's automatics," Hunter requested of Buck as he led the way in the direction Karissa and the deputy had taken. "The resources of whoever is after Karissa are staggering. If this person has backup personnel out there, I don't want to meet them weaponless."

When they intersected with Karissa and the deputy's route, the trail was unmistakable. Someone was losing blood, and droplets were visible along the way, here on a leaf, there on a branch. Quite possibly Karissa was still bleeding from the head wound. If Buck and Steggy and he hadn't put a stop to the attackers back at the road, the gunmen would have had no trouble finding their quarry. The path of the fleeing pair seemed to be erratic. Clearly, one or both of them was disoriented and staggering.

Please be okay. Please be okay. Hunter's heart filled his throat, strangling any verbalization of the chant that filled his head.

"There." Buck pointed toward a small open glade ahead.

Hunter rushed forward. The deputy lay on his side, clutching his right arm and moaning. His staring eyes appeared glazed and unfocused. Karissa sprawled on her face, lying perfectly still. A puddle of blood, redder than her hair, haloed her head.

SIX

Karissa drifted toward consciousness. A murmur of voices told her she wasn't alone here—wherever *here* was. And what was that annoying beeping sound that aggravated the pounding in her head?

Opening her eyes proved an intense struggle, but at last she achieved it and lay staring at a white ceiling. An antiseptic odor teased her nostrils, and she sneezed. The act speared shards of agony through her brain.

"She's awake!" exclaimed a male voice, familiar yet not well-known.

A man's head inserted itself between her and the ceiling, and a callused hand wrapped around one of hers. Piercing gray eyes studied her. "How are you doing, Karissa?"

Her mind scrambled to identify this guy with shaggy brown hair, wild beard, puckered scars around his left eye and left arm in a sling. Did she know him? Yes, oh yes. Her insides knotted as memories overlaid with residual terror crowded into her consciousness. Hunter Raines. He'd saved her more than once. But that didn't explain her current situation.

"How did I end up in the hospital?" Her voice came out a croak.

Her gaze traveled across the IV bags and tubes attached to her and moved on to the tray table at her bedside and beyond to a pair of guest chairs standing against the wall. The chairs were empty, which meant that the person who had been talking to Hunter was on the other side of her. She swiveled her gaze to the side. A doctor. His name tag said Dr. Werth, and he carried a stethoscope around his neck over his white coat. The man was tall and lean, and his distinguished-looking mop of gray hair, along with maturity lines on his face, put him somewhere in his fifties or sixties.

The doctor nodded toward Hunter. "Why don't you step out of the room while I examine her." The words emerged more of a command than a suggestion.

Hunter flattened his lips but obeyed. As his broad back disappeared behind a closing door, a pang gripped Karissa's middle. Why should she suddenly experience this sense of abandonment when she'd only known the guy for less than twenty-four hours? Well, depending on how long she'd been lying here unconscious.

"How's your head?" the doctor asked as he placed his stethoscope over her heart.

"Like a whole timpani section is holding practice in my brain," she rasped.

Her hand flew to her forehead, where she discovered bandages enveloping the entire circumference of her upper scalp. One spot near her temple stabbed pain when her fingers brushed across it. Okay, she'd taken a blow to the head, but how? Where? A car accident like the one that had taken her parents' lives? Seemed the most logical answer. Had the deputy's vehicle crashed? At least she'd survived her accident. Her parents hadn't made it.

"Here." Doctor Werth produced a plastic mug with a straw sticking out of it and put the end of the straw to her lips. "Take only a sip. We don't know how well you will keep things down yet."

She obediently sucked at the straw, and welcome fluid bathed her parched throat. All too soon, the doctor withdrew the mug.

"What happened?" she asked. "How long have I been out of it? What hospital am I in?"

"You're safe here at the Sacred Heart Medical Center in Eugene, Oregon. You've been here for around ten hours." The doctor frowned. "You don't remember the incident?"

"What incident?" Her tone had an edge to it, but too bad. Why wouldn't someone explain to her what was going on?

"What's the last thing you recall?" The doctor's smile was gentle...like she needed kid-glove handling.

Hardly reassuring when your doctor acted this concerned. All right, she'd play along. If she presented herself as strong—aware—maybe she'd start getting straight answers.

"Feeling safe at last in the deputy sheriff's car and allowing myself to drift off to sleep."

"Then you don't remember anything about being broadsided by a large SUV and assisting the injured deputy to flee into the forest?"

Karissa gasped and partially sat up, but a twist of

pain in her head forced her to subside onto the pillow. "We were attacked again?"

The doctor's frown deepened. "Apparently, but considering your concussion, I'm not surprised that you have no recollection of the event. Law enforcement will be disappointed, but they'll have to go on Hunter's testimony and what little the deputy remembers."

"The bad guys? Are they in custody?"

The doctor raised a forestalling hand. "I'm going to leave it to the legal authorities to answer those kinds of questions. You're safe here. A police officer is stationed outside your door, and your self-appointed protector, the one who was with you at the time of the accident, hovers over you like a mother hen."

A small smile tilted the corners of Karissa's lips. "He has that way about him."

For the first time, the doctor smiled, age lines crinkling the corners of his blue eyes. "Apparently, that young man saved your life and was injured in the process."

"Is that why he's wearing a sling on his arm?"

"He took a bullet to the bicep, but he'll be all right."

Karissa pressed her lips together. Should she be appalled that Hunter had been hurt on her account or grateful that he'd been there once more to stand between her and whoever was after her? Probably a whole bunch of both.

She gazed up at the doctor. "Would you send him in, please? I want to thank him."

She also wanted to pick his brain for a full account of the attack that she couldn't remember. If she could hang on to consciousness that long. The room was spinning, and that sip of water wasn't sitting so well in her stomach. Maybe she'd go ahead and close her eyes. Just for a second...

When conscious awareness next found Karissa and she opened her eyes, her room lights were dim and she was alone. Well, maybe not. Were those soft snores coming from nearby? She turned her head. Thankfully, the timpani section in her brain had gone home, and the pain had subsided to a mild throb.

Hunter sat in a guest chair, furry chin on his chest, mouth slightly agape. Yes, the snores originated with him. They were even kind of cute.

"Hey."

Her softly spoken word seemed to shoot electricity through him. He jerked and sat up straight. Then he grinned at her. The guy had a great smile that warmed her to her toes.

"Hey, yourself," he said. "The doc says you don't remember the attack on us on the road."

"Sorry. I don't remember anything about what put me in a hospital bed. What can you tell me?"

Hunter scooted his chair closer to her. She reached out her hand, and he cradled it in his own. His rich gray gaze sparked, and then his expression went shuttered. The retreat stung. Not for the first time, she sensed he was hiding something fundamental about himself. But what? Was he a criminal who'd been hiding out in Umpqua National Forest? No. That conclusion made no sense. A fugitive wouldn't have welcomed law enforcement presence at the biker bar. Still, there was something that cast a long shadow between Hunter and her.

Until she found out what it was, her trust in him could not be complete. She withdrew her hand from his.

Hunter cleared his throat and launched into a wild tale of being broadsided on the road by a large vehicle and the sheriff apparently abandoning them. Then there was a firefight between Hunter and their assailants, while she and the deputy escaped into the woods. The story raised the hairs on the back of her head. In this case, not remembering was a clear blessing.

But what about Kyle? A soft gasp left her lips.

"What is it?" Hunter leaned closer.

"Kyle. Is he all right? I know we left him with Starla and the ladies at the bar, but what has become of him since? He's my cousin Nikki's baby. I feel responsible. I—"

"He's fine."

Hunter's reassurance calmed her heart rate. "Is he still with Buck's wife?"

He shook his head. "Bitty boy is safe. I'll tell you more about him, but I first want to update you that our status in Nikki's murder and Kyle's supposed abduction has changed from suspects to victims."

"What a relief!" She exhaled a long breath. "How did that happen?"

Hunter grinned. "Almost as soon as we arrived at the hospital, a detective from the state police showed up looking for statements. You were out for the count, but he got an earful from me and Buck and the county sheriff's deputy. At that point, the sheriff was still on the missing list, and I haven't been updated since then about her. But as a result of our combined testimony, the detective seemed convinced that you are being targeted by whoever is behind the murder. He also seemed pretty impressed with your heroics in protecting Kyle. He said Kyle has been collected by family services and placed in a temporary foster home."

Karissa frowned and plucked at the sheet that covered her. "Poor Nikki. She'll never get to see her son grow up." She raised her eyes to meet Hunter's. "You know, I may be his only living relative…unless they can find someone on the father's side."

"Are you saying you'd like to have custody of him?" Hunter's brows climbed into his shaggy bangs.

"I'm saying… I don't know. A part of me would like nothing better, but there's still so much danger going on around me and no sign of a solution yet. I'm scared, Hunter. What if this never ends? Or it ends with me dead?"

"Don't talk like that." Hunter's tone was sharp. "The authorities are investigating, and you have a lot of people on your side. Me in particular. I'm not going to let anything happen to you."

"Why do you care so much? Until yesterday I was a stranger to you. I'd think you'd want to get as far away from me and my problems as possible—especially now that law enforcement can take it from here." She searched his face for answers he'd so far seemed unwilling to give.

Hunter looked away and combed his fingers through his beard. "I have something to tell you." He darted her a glance beneath lowered eyelids. "Something I probably should have told you right away."

"Yes?" Karissa prompted.

Whatever it was, she needed to know. What could

be so awful that the fearless Hunter Raines was hesitant to come straight out with it?

Hunter squared his shoulders, lifted his gaze to hers and opened his mouth, but the hospital room door suddenly whooshed wide and a husky figure filled the doorway.

"What on earth are you still doing in here, Mr. Raines?" The nurse's sharp tone chopped through the expectant atmosphere. "This young woman has a concussion and needs her rest. Out you go now, and no arguments."

"But—" Both Karissa and Hunter spoke at the same time.

"No. Arguments." Pinning Hunter beneath a glare, the nurse stood aside from the door and swept an arm toward the hallway.

Casting an apologetic look toward Karissa, Hunter rose. "Later then."

"You better follow through," she murmured to him.

He hung his head and walked out of the room as if the gallows held better prospects than the conversation that was to come.

Karissa bit her lip against frustration as the nurse checked her vital signs. How did anyone expect her to rest when she had so many questions unanswered?

Hunter slumped in an uncomfortable chair in the hospital waiting area opposite the nurse's station and near Karissa's room, where her door was plainly visible. Dark stares wafted toward him from the nurse at the desk. Other staff came and went from the nurses' station as part of their patient-care duties, but the charge nurse stayed put, doing paperwork and glaring daggers at him. No doubt she saw his perch in the waiting area as defiance of her authority. She'd made it clear when she booted him out of Karissa's room that he was supposed to be in his own room, which was up the hall.

He'd gone for a little while, but sleep eluded him because he wasn't able to keep watch over Karissa, and he hadn't been able to stay put in his hospital bed. Since Hunter's bullet wound had been a through and through with no shattered bones, his blood loss had been dealt with by a transfusion, and the possibility of infection had not seemed to materialize, they were going to discharge him in the morning anyway.

Ignoring the charge nurse's disapproval, he kept his gaze steady on Karissa's door. Dark stares, similar to the nurse's, flowed in his direction from the uniformed officer stationed there. Apparently, the officer didn't appreciate Hunter's vote of no-confidence, as evidenced by him taking up a position as back-up guard.

Too bad.

He didn't feel the least bit guilty about his implied insult to the guard's efficiency. Before his later ejection by the nurse, Hunter had been able to slip into Karissa's room right past the officer who'd become distracted chatting with an attractive young LPN. What kind of protection was that?

Besides which, after their recent experiences, Hunter wasn't inclined to trust someone just because of a uniform. He was going to speak to the man's supervisor tomorrow about the negligence, if that's all it was. Hunter returned the officer's glare with interest.

He could do a better job of keeping Karissa safe

and had already proven it…except now he'd caused her extreme distress with their interrupted conversation about his connection with her twin sister. Hunter's heart squeezed in on itself. How long did he have before Karissa found out he was potentially to blame for her sister's death? Not long. He'd soon have to tell her, or someone else would do it for him. The latter possibility sounded infinitely worse than the former. He shoved the dread down into a black hole in his mind.

Personal consequences didn't matter; Karissa's recovery did. Would his revelation hamper that recovery? Maybe he should hold off on baring his soul. But how could he do that when she already knew he had something to tell her?

At least he'd had one bit of good news since being admitted to the hospital. His brother, Jace, had showed up yesterday evening, safe and sound. It had actually felt great to have Jace read him the riot act for getting shot and generally behave like the smart-aleck kid brother trying to make like he wasn't scared out of his gourd at his big brother's close call with death.

Jace had also filled him in on the bomb threat at the Umpqua hydroelectric station that had, thankfully, turned out to be an empty scare. However, no one had responded to the smoke from Hunter's cabin because it was never reported—even by the volunteer spotters and the skeleton crew of personnel that had remained posted throughout the park despite the bomb threat. The federal park service was looking into why and how such a massive oversight had happened. Hunter had shared with Jace what Karissa had learned about their enemy having law enforcement in his pocket. Did the same go for park service personnel? Jace had left Hunter's hospital room with a bee under his bonnet to find out, but Hunter had warned him to be careful, because this person who was after Karissa seemed to have a long and deadly reach.

Now, Hunter was left with the precarious task of watching over a woman who likely would thrust him from her life the minute he told her his deepest, darkest secret. His personal attraction to Karissa on every level was completely irrelevant to his need to protect her. They had no future together because he couldn't undo any negligence that may have caused Karissa the loss of her twin. It came down to this: if he couldn't save Anissa, he was going to save Karissa. Maybe then he could live with himself for the rest of his life.

"Mr. Raines."

The nurse's sharp tones brought Hunter's attention around to her standing at his shoulder with her arms crossed and a scowl on her face. Evidently, her patience had completely run out. "You need to return to your room and stay there until morning. Ms. Landon is being well looked after."

"I beg to differ." Hunter sat up straight and met her stern stare. "I'm not questioning the medical care, you understand, but—"

"No buts. You're a patient here, so off you go to your proper bed."

"How about I discharge myself right now and just sit here the rest of the night?"

A smirk lengthened the nurse's lips. "Ah, but if you discharge yourself, then I will have to ask you to leave the premises."

Hunter groaned and scrubbed a hand across his face. When had his beard grown so straggly and wiry? He'd have to do something about that now that he was back in civilization. He didn't want to scare small children or get hassled for looking like a vagrant, which may be one reason he'd brought out the best in Nurse Pleasant, sarcasm fully intended. Of course, he couldn't shave the fur off completely, or he might still scare small children—with his burn scars.

"All right then." Hunter stood up and adjusted his sling. "I will go to my room if you will bring me a shaving kit that includes a small scissors."

"You're supposed to be sleeping."

"It'll be dawn in an hour or so. I'm used to being up by then, so I think I've done all the sleeping I'm going to do."

"Very well, sir." She shooed him up the hallway to his door then turned on her heel and all but stomped away.

Soon he was standing in front of his bathroom mirror snipping at the excessive beard, in between bouts of sticking his head out his door to make sure the cop was still guarding Karissa. He needed a haircut, too, but he didn't trust himself as his own barber to that extent. He wasn't doing such a great job at the beard trim, either, but at least he no longer looked like he'd been stranded on a deserted island for months and months—though the truth wasn't far off from that. And his eyes were different, too, since the last time he'd stared into them before he headed for his mountain retreat over a year ago. Then they'd been sunken in his head with a brooding sort of haunted look. Now they were cool and sharp with purpose, like they used to be.

Had the awakening come upon him unawares in the healing environment of the mountains or had Karissa and bitty boy brought it with their danger and their need? Hunter suspected the latter had completed the process begun by the former.

Two things he was going to do this morning—after he made sure the state police assigned someone more competent to Karissa's door—check that Kyle was safe and happy with his temporary foster family, and get his own cell phone so he could rejoin the twenty-first century. He had a feeling he was going to need any and every asset he could round up. This thing was far from over, and as much as the cops thought he should bow out now, his gut said Karissa still needed him. Maybe that was wishful thinking—but he was going to go with his gut anyway.

Speaking of gut, his stomach felt like he hadn't eaten since last week. He should get dressed and visit the vending machine to tide him over while he waited for breakfast and the doctor dropping by to discharge him, whichever came first. Not bothering with his shoes yet, Hunter ditched his sling and threw on the clean jeans and T-shirt Jace had gone out and bought to replace his bloody clothes. Then he stepped into the hallway.

His gaze lasered in on Karissa's doorway. No guard cop, and the halls were vacant of personnel—including the nurse's desk. No activity anywhere in view. In fact, the whole area was quiet—not the calm sort of quiet, but an ominous quiet.

Hunter burst into a sprint, his bare feet spanking

the cool tiles beneath them. A tiny part of his brain yelled caution, but if someone was going after Karissa, he might not have the spare seconds caution required. He hit her door with his good shoulder and catapulted inside to spot someone in a doctor's smock standing over Karissa.

Not Dr. Werth. This guy had a shaved-bald head, and the face-masked impostor was jabbing a needle into her arm.

SEVEN

A prick in her arm jerked Karissa awake from a sound sleep. The gloved hand holding the syringe that protruded from the crook of her elbow was suddenly ripped away, leaving the needle embedded in her flesh. The masked doctor who had been administering the drug began cursing and striking at an assailant with his fists. The attacker who had halted the injection defended himself with a strong right arm and a feeble left.

Oh, it was Hunter. No wonder it had taken her a few seconds to recognize him. He'd trimmed his beard away to a somewhat fashionable stubble, but his thick hair still swung around his broad shoulders. Why was he interfering with a doctor? And why was a doctor reacting with violence?

Chilling realization washed over her. The man who had been injecting something into her arm was no doctor. This was another attack from whoever was trying to kill her. If only she knew why she was marked for death. Her pulse rate fluttered and spiked.

The two men flailed at each other. Fists smacked flesh, and objects in the room crashed to the floor or flew against walls, but Karissa's gaze fixed on the syringe dangling from her arm. From the fluid level showing in the gauge, whatever the guy had been trying to give her appeared to still be in the tube—or at least most of it was. She reached across her body and, with cautious fingers, dislodged the needle from her flesh and flung the syringe away from her.

Surely, with all this racket, hospital staff must be on the way. And what about the officer that was supposed to be guarding her door? The thoughts floated hazily through Karissa's wounded head, but then a gunshot brought her bolt upright. The sudden movement stabbed white heat through her brain.

Blackness edged her vision, but she made out the figures of Hunter and the face-masked man struggling for possession of a firearm. Both men's hands were wrapped around the weapon with the gun barrel pointed upward.

Another report sent a bullet into the ceiling. The fake doctor's back was toward her, and Hunter's head topped the guy's shoulder, facing her. From the pallor of Hunter's flesh, the gritted teeth and the sweat glistening on his forehead, she had to guess he was weakening, no doubt due to the wound he was still recovering from. She had to help somehow.

Head pounding and heart flailing against her ribs, Karissa slipped out of bed, gaze searching for some kind of weapon to defend herself—and her rescuer. *There!* The IV pole that had been left in her room after the IV port had been removed from her hand. She hefted it and gave the fake doctor a hearty whack across the back. The man grunted and attempted to turn toward her. Hunter took advantage of the distraction and flung the man against the wall. The pistol fell to the floor. The fake doctor turned and ran from the room, pulling the door shut behind him. Hunter leaped as if to follow him but abruptly halted and swiveled toward her.

"Are you...all right?" His question emerged in winded puffs.

One corner of his mouth was split open and oozing blood, and a red stain was spreading across the white bandage on his left arm.

"I'm fine," she managed, but with a quaver in her voice. "It looks like your arm is reinjured, though."

The door banged open, and Karissa jumped then froze, staring. A young, uniformed police officer filled the opening. His pale blue eyes had a glazed look, unfocused, and a trickle of red flowed from beneath the hairline at his temple down to his chin and dripped onto his uniform shirt.

"Some doctor clocked me on the head and threw me in the supply closet," he said, words slurring. "What's going on in here?"

Karissa sank onto the bed. "Someone tried to kill me. Again. Would someone please tell me why this is happening?" Her question came out with a hint of a wail.

Hunter shook his shaggy head. "I wish I knew."

Multiple rushing footsteps approached, and hospital personnel flooded into the room. Karissa was ushered immediately to another room so the authorities could process her former room as a crime scene. Hopefully, she'd know soon what substance her assailant had been trying to inject into her vein. From her new bed, while a nurse checked her blood pressure and pulse, she offered a weak smile to Hunter, who was perched in his self-appointed guard post in a chair at her bedside. He reached out and squeezed her hand. Warmth traveled up her arm from the comforting human connection and delivered a slight thaw to the chill gripping her core.

An intern was cleaning his arm wound and clucking at him that he needed new stitches.

"You'll have to do it right here," Hunter said. "I'm not leaving this room. Where were you people when Karissa was being attacked?"

The intern glanced at her, gaze sheepish. "Multiple false summons all over the wing." Then he shook his head at Hunter. "I'll be back shortly with sutures for your arm."

The intern exited the room.

Karissa punched the mattress of her bed. "This is too ridiculous! I've lost all my family, except baby Kyle and…" Her voice fought the sudden tightness in her throat. "And I don't have a clue who is masterminding this or why."

"We'll figure it out."

She met his gray gaze. "I feel safer with you than with anybody else. But I can't make sense of it. You still haven't told me. Why do you care enough to risk your life for me?"

Hunter's tan faded as the blood receded from his face. He sucked in an audible breath then his expression hardened as if he'd reached a resolve. "You deserve to know. I was a firefighter before—"

"All righty, we need to get some statements here," an authoritative male voice announced.

Karissa ripped her gaze away from Hunter's intense

face. She turned her head toward the door to find a plainclothes detective flashing his badge at them.

"Are you okay, miss?" The detective pocketed his shield.

"I—I guess so. For now, anyway."

The lanky, middle-aged man pulled up a chair on the other side of her bed from Hunter. "I've met your friend here." He nodded toward Hunter then fixed his gaze on Karissa. "I'm Detective Sykes from the Oregon State Police. I was already nearly here when I got the call about another attack on you, Miss Landon. Tell me about that."

Volleying between her and Hunter, with a few questions from the detective interjected, the morning's story was fleshed out. At the end of it, Sykes clucked his tongue.

"Another narrow escape." The detective squinted hard eyes at Hunter. "You keep stepping between this woman and the people who are after her."

"What do you mean by that?" Hunter matched the detective's stare.

"Just that you're taking a lot of risks, sir." The man offered a bland smile and then turned his attention on Karissa. "Now, I was told by your doctor, who wouldn't let me talk to you yesterday even after you had awakened, that you are experiencing retrograde amnesia due to your head injury. He said you can't remember anything about the incident where you were broadsided by attackers on the road. Have you remembered anything at all yet?"

She shook her head and winced at the painful protest from her bruised brain. "No, sir, I haven't. The doctor said that I may never recover that sliver of memory. I can remember everything up to the attack on the road, but if you need to know what happened to land me and Hunter in the hospital, you'll have to talk to him."

The detective frowned then raised an eyebrow at Hunter. "All righty, Mr. Raines. We'll start with you, because your memories are complete. Take it from the top and run through everything you know about events beginning two days ago through this morning. I've studied the statements you gave yesterday, but I'd like to hear it all again. Ms. Landon, please feel free to interject any details Mr. Raines may skip over in regard to events prior to the SUV broadsiding the deputy's car."

Karissa lay very still and listened with all her might to the details of a fascinatingly scary account of the past two days of her life, most of which she remembered and a little of which she didn't. Hunter did an excellent job of highlighting all the pertinent details, so she had little to insert. However, at one point she sat up on her elbows.

"Kyle. Is he still all right? Is he safe? A fresh attack against me makes me wonder if there have been any further attempts on Kyle."

The detective held up a forestalling hand. "When I checked this morning, Miss Landon, Kyle was doing fine in foster care."

"Then there no relatives to take him? I mean, I know I'm the last on Nikki's mother's side, but I'm not all that familiar with her father's side."

Sykes frowned. "Apparently, no one has been located yet. Don't worry. We don't think whoever is after you is targeting the infant. Though we are keeping an eye on him, it makes more sense to think he was a collateral issue to pursuing *you*."

Karissa subsided onto her pillow. "You mean, *I* put Kyle in danger by snatching him up? Should I have just left him in his crib in the house where his mother was murdered?"

Hunter touched the hand she had fisted around the sheet. "I don't think that was a good alternative." He switched his attention to Sykes. "Detective, did your people ever catch up with the sheriff who abandoned us to that attack on the road and the two crooks she had in her back seat?"

Sykes frowned. "We did. The sheriff's vehicle was found in a ravine not far ahead of where you were ambushed. It took us a while to locate it because the vehicle had been covered over with brush. The sheriff was awake but groggy with a large goose egg on the back of her head. She was handcuffed to her own steering wheel. Claims she has no idea how the two suspects got to her, but they were gone."

Karissa groaned. "So, the two gunmen who tried to kidnap me—one of whom killed my cousin—are on the loose again?"

"Sounds like it." Hunter's tone was thin.

"At least the sheriff is okay," Karissa said. "And she wasn't in on the plot."

Hunter frowned. "We don't know that. The scene could have been staged to make her look innocent."

"Don't go leaping to conclusions about law enforcement personnel," Sykes barked, scowling at Hunter.

"Not leaping." He answered the detective's anger with a bland look. "I understand you defending your own, but I'm trying to keep an open mind to possibilities when we know from one of the bad guys that some kind of corruption is going on."

Sykes grunted. "I'll believe that when it's proven." He turned the page in his small notebook and focused on Karissa. "You have no idea who might be after you or why?"

She shook her head. "I'm clueless, which makes me feel as helpless as little Kyle. I mean, I've been out of the country for the past two years on the mission field in Belize. The conditions there were challenging at times, and some of the neighborhoods could be really scary, and yet I seem to be less safe after returning to my home country than I was in a third-world country. Can anyone explain that anomaly to me?"

She glared from Hunter to Detective Sykes. Both men held their silence behind sober expressions.

She sighed. "It was a rhetorical question, anyway. It's just so strange that first my parents were killed in a car accident and then Anissa died in a fire right before I left the country." The awful words tasted like bile on her tongue. She turned toward Hunter. "You started to tell me you used to be a firefighter. Were you stationed anywhere in Oregon? Did you ever hear anything about the fire that took my sister?"

If she'd put a gun to his head, Hunter couldn't have looked any more terrified. No, she'd seen him handle someone with a gun and deadly intent. The man didn't scare easily. The horror in his wide eyes was more on par with being told that everything and everyone he cared about was being ripped from him. Sort of similar to the way Karissa was feeling about all the losses piling up around her. What was he hiding that could possibly be that bad?

* * *

Hunter squeezed his eyes shut. The moment of truth. He'd known it was coming but had hoped against hope that he would not have to be the one to personally tell her of his role in Anissa's death. Of course, his prayer to be far away from Karissa when this moment came had been pure selfishness. God wasn't going to allow that. Hunter had to look her in the eye and tell her the truth, then take whatever condemnation and fury she poured out on him. If he wasn't already starting to care about her so much on a personal level—against his better judgment—he might be able to weather her contempt. Couldn't be helped. He opened his eyes.

Karissa's gaze was still fixed on him, wide and expectant. Hunter opened his mouth, but the detective's cell phone chose that moment to ring.

The man checked the screen and held up a finger as he rose from the chair. "Just a sec. I've got to take this."

Hunter waved him off, and the man hustled from the room. Actually, not having a third-party audience might make the next few minutes easier, but not by much.

"Until a couple of years ago, I was a firefighter in Portland," he began in a low voice.

"That's where Anissa and I were living," Karissa interrupted. "Not together, though. She had a little house, and I lived in an apartment, but we both worked in the city and saw each other quite often." Karissa's tone had turned warm and eager in the recollection of happier days.

Hunter's heart twisted. "Hear me out."

"I will." She rolled onto her side, reached over and touched the scarred side of his face, her expression tender. "But let me say this first. You may well be the bravest man I've ever met. I've seen you in action saving my life and little Kyle's more than once. If that's what you were like with us then I can imagine you were like that as a firefighter. I suspect that's how you got those burns—putting yourself at risk—so if anyone can explain with empathy what happened to my sister, you're the guy, so go ahead."

Hunter swallowed hard. "I'm the guy, all right," he rasped. "I got these trying to get Anissa out of her bedroom on the second floor—"

Karissa let out a small shriek, eyes going wide. "You were there at that very fire? Oh, of course! I just made the connection—a firefighter in Portland, burned two years ago. It must have been a horrible shock when I landed on your doorstep in the backwoods. You were injured on behalf of my sister, and now I've put you through the wringer again. You probably wish you'd never heard of the Landon family."

"It's not that at all," Hunter rushed onward. "I am so thankful to have another chance to help someone in your family when I failed to save Anissa."

"You mustn't feel bad." Her gaze was compassionate. "Clearly, you tried your best—even to the point of getting hurt yourself."

"I *did* try my best, but it wasn't good enough because some equipment failed. Instead of holding us until we could get pulled to safety, the harness broke when the floorboards gave way, and we got dumped into the worst of the blaze on the first floor. I lived only because the fire-retardant mattress from Anissa's bedroom fell on top of me."

"Survivor's guilt."

"Not at all. You haven't heard the rest of the story. The equipment failure may have been my f—"

"Miss Landon, Mr. Raines." The detective's voice boomed as he strode back into Karissa's room. "I hate to be the bearer of bad news, but I figured you'd want to know. Kyle has disappeared from his foster home. Every available unit is out looking for him now, and we've issued an Amber alert. I'm so sorry."

A wordless cry broke from Karissa's throat, and her face turned deathly pale.

Hunter surged to his feet. "You're sorry? Clearly, you underestimated the threat to the little guy."

"It's a possibility we considered, which is why we had an unmarked surveillance unit stationed outside the foster family's house, but someone got to the child in spite of our vigilance."

Hunter glared at the detective. The detective glared back.

The intern who had treated Hunter's arm glided into the room bearing a suture kit and wearing a big smile. "Let's get that wound restitched so we can discharge you."

"Best idea I've heard all day," Hunter pronounced and plopped into his chair. "I've got a baby to find."

Sykes jabbed a finger at him. "You need to stay out of our way and let us do our job, Mr. Raines."

"It's an Amber alert, right?" He let the intern get to work. "Anybody can look for the kid." Checking in on what contacts Buck might have in the area and activating them to look for Kyle wasn't a move he felt he needed to mention to the detective, especially when he planned to see if any of those contacts had a firearm they could loan him. "I think it's pretty safe to say that Karissa and I may be the people left in this world who care about him the most."

"That's for sure." Karissa nodded, jaw firming. Her green gaze flashed as color rushed back into her face. "It sounds like I might be his only living relative. I'm going to look, too."

"No, you're not!" The detective and Hunter spoke in unison.

The intern stared down at her. "You have a serious concussion. If you try too much activity too quickly, you could not only pass out at any moment, but you may aggravate any existing brain damage. At the very least, you would delay healing."

"What he said." Hunter seconded the intern with a stern finger stabbed in Karissa's direction.

"Plus," added Sykes, "you're under police protection until we discover and stop whoever is making these attempts on your life." The detective sent a grim stare toward Hunter. "I promise we'll have *two* officers at the door from now on."

"You'd better," Hunter grated out.

EIGHT

Heart rate jumping all over the place, Karissa studied the medium-size, burnt-orange purse that had been laid on her tray table moments earlier by one of the officers guarding her door. "Here you go," she had said with a grin. "Detective Sykes authorized me to return this to you. It's been gone through—sorry—but nothing in here was deemed of evidentiary value so you can have your handbag back." Then she'd turned and left the room to resume her post.

Karissa sat up on the edge of her bed with her feet dangling over the side and swiped away a sheen of moisture that had popped out on her upper lip at sight of her purse. Her kidnapper in the woods had told her that her handbag and her car were in the possession of those who wanted her dead. How had the purse come back into police custody? Had her kidnapper lied? To what purpose? Or was this sudden return of her property another clue taunting her with the possibility that members of law enforcement were bought and paid for by her powerful nameless, faceless enemy? That possibility threw a taint over her bag. Touching it, much less opening it, seemed like a risky act, yet what choice did she have but to examine the contents to confirm that everything inside was indeed hers and nothing had been added or taken away?

"Don't be a coward," she whispered to herself under her breath.

It might have been nice to have a friend like Hunter present to walk through this potential minefield with her, but he'd taken off like a scalded cat as soon as his wound was freshly sutured. Now he was off looking for Kyle. Her heart cheered him on, but where he would start the hunt for the baby, she had no clue.

Firming her jaw, she reached for the bag. Item by item, she emptied the contents and laid them out on the tray table in front of her. A mirrored compact. A small zipper pouch containing basic articles of makeup. A wide-toothed comb, needed to help tame her wild red locks—probably something that badly needed doing after all the racing around in the woods and then lolling in bed. A lady's wallet containing a little cash, her driver's license and a credit card. A travel-size first aid kit, complete with adhesive bandages, antiseptic wipes and a small container of acetaminophen. A key ring holding the key to her small apartment in Portland and her car keys—where *was* her car, by the way? A few odds and ends like dental floss and lip gloss. And her cell phone. All of her possessions seemed present and accounted for.

She grabbed up her cell and clutched it to her chest like she'd discovered buried treasure. Now she could reach out and contact someone like…who? Nikki was dead with their reunion never having taken place. Her precious Belizean friends were thousands of miles away. Of course, there were a few old friends and former co-workers in her contact list from before she left for the mission field who she was sure wouldn't mind hearing from her, but to what point and what would she say?

Hi, I'm calling to hear a friendly voice because an unknown enemy is trying to kill me, and I don't know why. If anything like that popped out of her mouth, they would think she'd lost her mind.

The only person she really wanted to call was Hunter, and she didn't have his number—if he even owned a cell phone. She'd seen no sign of one when they were on the run in the forest. Not that they would have had service out there anyway.

Karissa frowned. She *could* contact her pastor. Her church had helped support her on the mission field, and they had an awesome prayer group with whom she'd often shared prayer needs. If this situation wasn't a prayer need, she didn't know what was. She brought up her contacts and tapped the listing for her pastor's church office.

The call rang and rang and then went to voice mail. Karissa's throat constricted against tears that wanted to fall. This wasn't the sort of situation about which she could leave any kind of coherent detailed voice message. The beep came for her to leave her message.

"Hi, this is Karissa Landon," she managed to rasp out. "Would you add my name to the prayer list? I'm having a little trouble. God knows what's going on. Just…please pray for me."

She choked over the final words and tapped to end

the call. Could she have sounded more pitiful if she tried?

Her cell suddenly buzzed harshly and vibrated in her hand. She dropped it as if stung. The cell's protective case hit the tile floor with a soft *clunk*. Gingerly, holding on to her woozy head with one hand, Karissa eased off the bed, reached down and retrieved the phone. Scarcely daring to breathe, she awakened the screen again. The number one next to the messaging icon told her that a new text had come in. In a couple of taps, the message, which originated from an unfamiliar number, slapped her in the face.

Remember the Golden Days?
You have two hours
Or an innocent pays the price.
No cops, no fireman.
Your car is in the parking garage.
The way is clear.
Come to me now.

The Golden Days Care Center? How did her enemy know about her family's connection to that senior care facility? Then, again, how did whoever it was always seem to know details of her life? This person had somehow known she would be visiting her cousin Nikki and had gotten there ahead of her—with tragic consequences.

Waves of cold followed by waves of heat washed over her body. She was afraid—terrified even—she admitted, but she was also angry. Who did this joker think he was, playing God with people's lives?

God, You know what's going on here and who is behind it. Help!

Her heart rate settled as if under a calming hand. Such a brief and simple cry for help, and yet it reminded her who had her in the palm of His hand. That sure and certain knowledge did not lessen the danger, but it did remind her to trust the outcome of events into His loving care. Nevertheless, her course of action was clear. The safety of her cousin's innocent baby came first. Kyle's sweet face appeared in her mind's eye—all the motivation she needed to ignore her fears and take action.

With delicate care, Karissa removed her hospital gown and dressed herself in the clothes that had been placed in her closet. The collar of her shirt bore blood-stains, but her long hair would cover those. Standing in front of the mirror in the bathroom, she unwound the bandage from her head. A large yellowing bruise marred her temple on one side. She lifted a bright auburn lock and spotted a shaved area and a sutured cut only an inch or so back from her hairline. Her head ached, but a recent dose of extra-strength Tylenol had blunted the edges of the pain.

What now? Walk out the door as if her two guards didn't exist?

She frowned at her reflection. The message had said the way was clear for her to leave. The guards must be gone. One way to find out.

Karissa repacked everything in her purse but retained her car keys in her hand. With the other hand, she snatched up her handbag and peeked out the door of the hospital room. The beast who had Kyle was right.

No uniformed officers stood guard. Further proof that she didn't know who in law enforcement she could trust.

A nurse at the main desk was consulting charts and didn't lift her head, nor did the housekeeper look up from counting towels on her cart as Karissa made her soft-footed way to the elevator. Were they in her enemy's employ, too? Apparently, anyone could be.

Minutes later, she reached the parking garage. She pressed the unlock button on her key fob and was rewarded by a pair of lights flashing at her an aisle over from where she was standing. Hauling in deep breaths against the enormity of her course of action compared to her frailty, Karissa took steady, deliberate steps toward her little car.

Her hand closed around the Toyota's door handle just as iron fingers gripped her upper arm and whirled her about. Gulping back a scream, she stared up into eyes of fury.

"Where do you think you're going?" Hunter demanded through gritted teeth.

Karissa let out a small whimper, and he almost felt bad for being so harsh. Almost. What was this woman thinking in ditching her protective detail—how had she done that, anyway?—and taking off on her own while in the grip of a concussion?

"It said you can't come." Her words gushed forth. "Kyle's safety is on the line. They'll hurt him if they see you or the cops."

"Whoa! Slow down. What *it* are you talking about?"

"The text." She pulled a cell phone from the orange purse she seemed suddenly to have acquired.

Scowling, he read the message and then cocked a brow at Karissa. "You thought haring off alone was the thing to do in response to this threat?"

"It was the *only* thing to do." She drew herself up to every micrometer of her petite height and glared at him.

If the situation were less dire, Hunter might have smiled at the ferocity. Then again, he'd witnessed her courage and endurance. Anyone would do well not to underestimate this one. Of its own volition, his hand reached out and brushed her cheek with his fingertips. Her eyes widened, and his breath caught.

He snatched his hand away and cleared his throat. "I don't care what the instructions are. You're not going alone."

A growl left her throat. "There's no time for this delay. I have to be at the Golden Days Care Center in Portland in less than two hours."

"Portland I get because that's where those two goons were taking you after they kidnapped you in the woods. You're from there. I'm from there, too. Not that I think my home stomping grounds mean anything to this creep. Maybe your enemy is from there, too. But why choose some random nursing home as a meeting ground?"

Karissa crossed her arms over her chest. "I don't know specifically, but my grandmother spent her last years there. Our family used to visit her often."

Hunter let out a whistle under his breath. "This low-life really knows details about your life."

"Apparently, and that intimacy scares me as much as anything, but we really don't have time to waste in speculation right now."

"Then we'd better get going. Thankfully, Interstate 5 should provide smooth sailing. Oh, and I'm driving." He held out his hand for the keys.

With a long sniff, she surrendered them. They got into the Toyota, and Hunter headed the vehicle out of the parking garage. At least the feel of the compact Ruger LCP handgun tucked in the waistband of his jeans offered some margin of comfort. Buck had come through with a friend who had a firearm he could borrow on the fly. Hunter had also acquired a new cell phone—his hello to modern civilization after so long on the backside of nowhere.

He glanced over at Karissa's stony profile. "Since we have a little time on our hands, you can explain to me in detail how you came to be in possession of that purse and phone and how you managed to escape your guards. I shudder to think what your situation would be right now if I didn't happen to be returning to the hospital in the nick of time to catch sight of you and tail you to your car."

"I'd be on the interstate already," she snipped. "Now that you're hitching along, I have no idea how to ensure Kyle's safety."

"What ability did you think you had to do that all by yourself, anyway?"

He caught her giving him a sidelong look. "You're not going to call the police, are you?"

"Not with their current track record."

She seemed to deflate as she slumped forward against her seat belt. "Good, because I'm not sure if the policewoman who gave me my purse this morning was lying about Detective Sykes releasing it to me, or if Sykes is in on whatever is going on, or if there's some other scenario I haven't considered yet."

"Explain."

Karissa tersely told him about the return of her purse and the troubling inconsistency with what her kidnapper had told her about the purse and car being in her enemy's custody, as well as the fact that both officers who had been guarding her door were missing when she left the hospital.

"Somebody has a long reach and deep pockets to keep pulling this stuff off," Hunter said. "Let's return to the obvious fact that the mastermind behind this vendetta knows your family well. What enemies have the Landons made over the years?"

"I honestly have no idea. I mean, I know my dad was a shark in the business world. I suppose he might have ruffled a few feathers."

"*Was* a businessman? Oh, yes, you did say something when Sykes was with us about an accident that claimed your parents' lives."

Karissa frowned and shook her head. "He and my mom were killed in a car crash a few months before the fire that took Anissa. Some hit-and-run driver came out of nowhere and T-boned them."

T-boned? Hunter's heart lurched in his chest. "Are you sure that crash was an accident?"

She grimaced and pressed her palms to her temples. "I'm not sure of anything right now. What about the fire?" Her gaze swiveled toward him, eyes wide. "The fire marshal ruled the blaze accidental—an electrical short in the kitchen wall."

Hunter rolled his shoulders. "Yeah, I remember."

He gritted his teeth against releasing another word. This was not the time to finish telling her the story of his culpability. She needed to go on trusting him, because he was all she had on her side right now.

"The verdict of an electrical short always felt off to me." Karissa frowned. "Anissa was a safety stickler. She had that home inspected with a fine-toothed comb before she bought it. No electrical problems were identified. I said that to the fire marshal at the time."

"I know the standard response to that objection—things hidden behind walls can be missed," Hunter said, but in light of recent events, the stock answer rang hollow.

What if none of the tragedies that had befallen Karissa's family members before she left for Belize were accidental?

"Could we be right in suspecting that someone has it in for my family?" She voiced in breathless tones the question Hunter had been mulling. "Did my leaving for Belize preserve my life for a time, but now that I'm back, I'm a target again? That's so nuts. I sound paranoid."

"You have every reason to be paranoid." He reached over and gripped one of her petite hands in his. Her fingers felt cold, as if a chill were coursing through her veins. "How do we find out who might want to destroy your family?"

Her hand squeezed his, and her eyes blinked rapidly as she stared straight ahead at the ribbon of I-5 they had just entered. "Maybe he or she will answer that question when we get to Portland, because there's no time for any research." She disengaged her fingers from his and crossed her arms, hugging herself. "This whole theory is so horrible it makes me wonder if Nikki was killed because I contacted her. Maybe her death is my fault."

Hunter fixed his eyes on the road. "None of this is your fault. One of the vilest ironies of evil is that the good folks tend to blame themselves for it happening, while the real perpetrators often couldn't care less."

She glanced at him from under her lashes. "That's actually pretty profound. I've never thought about it that way."

He squirmed under her warm gaze. She wouldn't admire him if she knew that he could well be one of the perpetrators that had caused her grief—but not on purpose and certainly not callously. Would he ever know the truth about whether or not he neglected that equipment inspection? But if he had done the inspection like he thought he remembered, why did the equipment fail? His secret was choking him, but he couldn't afford to distract her with the truth. Not in this moment. She'd send him packing, and he couldn't have that. Therefore, he was stuck keeping his mouth shut—for the time being. She needed to go on allowing him in her life, until the situation was resolved and she and bitty boy were safe. If only he could guarantee such a happy ending. They were driving straight into a trap, and he had no clue how to spring it without them being crushed in its maw.

NINE

Karissa dug around in the glove compartment, found a car phone charger and plugged her dying phone into it. She couldn't have the battery dead if Kyle's abductor wanted to contact her again. Now, what was she going to do to ditch this guy who was determined to protect her? Did she even want to ditch him? Not really, but his presence put the baby at risk. Surely he realized that much. She hazarded a sidelong look in Hunter's direction.

His intense gray gaze was fixed on the endless ribbon of interstate unfolding in front of them. They whizzed through flatlands, up and down rolling hills, and between stands of pine trees with occasional distant backdrops of higher elevations. They would reach Salem soon, and after that, Portland would quickly loom before them.

"What's your plan?" she demanded.

"First thing? Get you to the Golden Days on time. I'll stop and pile out about a block away from the place, but know this." He shot her a hard glance. "You may feel like you're walking in there alone, but you won't be. Somehow, I'll stay close, but I'm going to have to wing that part. Okay?"

"What are you? Some kind of master of disguise now? International spy? Man of intrigue?" Her laugh came out brittle. "I didn't know they taught that stuff in firefighter school."

Hunter snorted. "Hardly. I'm just a guy determined not to let evil win…this time."

His last two words came out so weighted they seemed to hit Karissa somewhere deep in her chest. He wasn't speaking in general. He was referring to a specific instance when he felt like evil had won. Would he ever expand on that thought? Now was not the time for the discussion.

She rubbed the side of her head. "That's the start of a plan, anyway. More than I had. Pretty much, I figure I'm going to do what I'm told until somehow we get Kyle to safety."

"We're on the same page on that, but I don't think we can be satisfied with recovering Kyle. Until we get to the bottom of what's going on and whoever is behind this is in custody, we're not home free."

"You keep saying *we*, but it's me they're after. Maybe after we get Kyle away from his kidnappers, I should return to Belize. Whoever this is didn't come after me there."

"There's no guaranteeing they won't do that now that they've exposed their intentions toward you and they're no longer trying to make whatever happens to you look accidental."

Karissa let out a long sigh. "Sometimes I wish you didn't make so much sense."

"How's the head?"

"Hurts, but I no longer feel like I'm going to pass out with every movement."

As they entered the city of Salem, traffic became thicker, slowing their progress. Karissa shifted in her seat, glancing at the time showing on her phone.

"Portland's less than an hour away," Hunter said. "We'll make it. In fact, we're going to do a quick pit stop and grab a little helpful gear."

In spite of her heated protests, her self-appointed escort pulled off I-5 and proceeded to an electronics store in a high-end strip mall.

"Trust me and give me five minutes," he said as he opened the vehicle door, gaze locked with hers.

Karissa opened her mouth to protest but stopped any words coming out. The fact was she *did* trust this guy. She closed her mouth and nodded. He grinned, and warmth spread through her heart. He was back in less than five minutes and handed her an oval object dangling from a lanyard.

"Put that around your neck but conceal it under your clothes. It's a GPS tracker. It's small but would be highly uncomfortable to put into a shoe. You could keep it in your pocket, but it could too easily fall out. Or you could put it in your purse, but what if the enemy takes your purse away? The lanyard seemed to me like the handiest solution."

"I accept your logic."

"I've already synced it to my phone so I can know where you are without seeing you."

"But couldn't we just install one of those tracker apps on my phone rather than using a separate device?"

"Good question. I'm operating on the assumption that your phone will be one of the first things taken away from you by an enemy. This tracker will be separate and concealed."

A little thrill—part fear, part a weird sense of excitement—shot through Karissa. Who would ever have pictured her ordinary little self in a situation that required such subterfuge?

"Thanks." She put the lanyard around her neck and hid the cord and device under her clothing.

"Try not to think about it being there or grip or touch the device. That would give away its presence to anyone watching."

"Oops! Sorry." She pulled her hand away from the tracker.

Hunter chuckled then sobered. "Come to think of it, I never asked you if you found anything unusual in your purse after you were given it back."

"I went through everything, item by item. Nothing was missing, and nothing was added. I think they just wanted me to have my phone back so they could contact me."

He nodded then pursed his lips. "Hand me your phone. Those killers had the device in their custody for a while. I'm not an expert and don't have any sophisticated tech equipment available to test for anything beyond the ordinary, but I can certainly check to see if they downloaded any of the usual tracking apps. Besides, I want to put my number in your contacts."

Karissa complied, and Hunter scrolled and tapped and clucked for a few seconds then handed it back to her. "I don't see any of the common apps people use, but that doesn't mean they might not have installed something that isn't obvious. However, only law enforcement with a duly executed warrant could track you by involving cell company personnel to triangulate cell tower pings."

"That's hardly reassuring when we know our enemy has strings on law enforcement personnel."

Hunter frowned. "True but arranging for that kind of tracking is more involved than getting a crooked cop to pull some off-the-books antics."

Karissa sighed. "We may have to take it on faith and hope that I'm not being tracked that way, because I have to hang on to this phone and keep it on as long as Kyle's kidnappers might communicate with me through it."

With a bleak nod, Hunter put the car in gear and headed them back to the interstate. The rest of the trip seemed both eternal and all too quick as Portland swallowed them up in its traffic and tall buildings with snow-capped Mount Hood looming in the distance. Following her directions, Hunter brought them close to the Golden Days Care Center. True to his word, he pulled over and got out a little more than a block away from the facility.

"Wait!" she called after him as she climbed out of the passenger seat.

He turned and gazed at her with those fathoms-deep gray eyes.

She swallowed hard. "How do we know they're not watching us right now?"

"We don't, but I doubt it. Makes more sense for them to spend their resources on placing watchers on the

Golden Days property. You can be pretty sure you'll be under surveillance when you get there."

"Okay. Thanks… I think." A soul-deep shiver ran through her.

He must have detected the shudder, because he strode toward her and wrapped her in his arms. "I've got your back, remember?"

She nodded against his sturdy chest. Something in the calm assurance of his words and the strength of his embrace communicated itself to her core, and a fresh steadiness took hold. This man grounded her and touched something deep inside her in a way that none other had ever done. What would it be like to have the chance to see what might come of the mutual attraction that continued to grow between them? She shoved the question away. Not the time for useless speculation.

"I'm all right now." She stepped away from him, instantly regretting the loss of his strong arms around her.

With a nod in his direction, Karissa got behind the wheel of her Toyota and watched Hunter walk away. She swallowed deeply against the lump in her chest. Her hand went to the tracker resting against her breastbone then she quickly snatched it away and gripped the steering wheel in both fists.

"Okay, God. Help me to keep my eyes on You."

With her whispered prayer, she put the car into gear and directed her little vehicle up the street and into the parking lot of the two-story, country club–like eldercare home. Nothing but the best for her dad's mother. After all, Henry Landon could afford it—well, at least until after he died and it was discovered that he was in debt up to his eyeballs. While he was alive, his next slick deal was the only thing standing between his family and bankruptcy. So, of course, after he was dead the whole fake business empire collapsed and left his daughters to clean up a pile of financial ruins. Karissa shook off the old and useless hurt and yanked her mind back to the critical present.

She parked the vehicle near the back of the lot, eyeing the sprawling, manicured grounds and tastefully ornate buildings. At the moment, these plush surroundings contained more personal danger for her than if she stood all alone in the middle of a crime-riddled neighborhood. Where did she go now?

Her phone buzzed, and she gasped then grabbed it up and gazed at the message.

You remember the room.

She did. She also remembered the stilted visits with a wrinkled, heavily made-up, fancily dressed woman who received the kindness and service of the staff as if she was entitled to it all and much more. But then, Grandma had always been a chilly and distant woman, demanding of others, indulgent of self. Old age hadn't changed her. Maybe that's where Dad got his habit of taking people for granted, treating them like objects, including his own family.

Karissa closed her eyes and took in several deep breaths. She'd determined long ago to forgive her father—even before he died so tragically.

Gripping her purse, Karissa opened her car door and began the trek toward what could be her end. Sure, her destination looked like a pair of welcoming glass doors flanked by cheerful flower beds, but for her, the portals could be the gateway to death. Only one way to find out—march on into the belly of the beast.

In another step, her phone buzzed, and she halted under a maple tree that shaded an intersection of two sidewalks. Hand shaking, she drew the phone from her purse and frowned at the screen.

Memory care wing

That's right. This place had a separate memory-care unit for residents with severe forms of dementia. Why the change of direction midstream, she had no idea. Perhaps merely to keep her off balance, but she had no inclination to question whoever had baby Kyle. It was creepy enough just to sense that hostile eyes seemed to be watching her every move since she arrived on campus. She prayed that Hunter was as good at hiding his presence here in the urban jungle as he had been at stealth in the forest. Or, at least, that the surveillance was so focused on her they might miss Hunter. If not, he was in as much danger as she was.

Turning on her heel, Karissa took the adjacent sidewalk that headed toward a sprawling, single-story building separate from the rest of the facility. The extra distance consumed an excruciating eternity. Her back itched as if a target were painted on it, and her breastbone tingled where the tracking device bounced gently against it. The heat of the sun from the outside and the heat of unrelenting fear from the inside conspired to send droplets of perspiration from her scalp down the sides of her face. In front of the partially glassed doors of the memory-care unit, she scrubbed at the moisture with her palms and squared her shoulders.

She opened a door into an entry foyer then went through a set of security doors into an elegantly appointed and air-conditioned seating area. The sudden chill sent a shiver through her. To one side of the entry stood a discreetly positioned reception desk. Directly ahead of her, a middle-aged woman holding a clipboard beamed a hundred-watt smile in her direction.

"You must be Larissa Watkins," clipboard woman gushed. "Your father described you perfectly. I'm Mrs. Hancock, and I'll be conducting your tour today."

Karissa froze, gaping at the exuberantly friendly woman. Her brain fought to wrap itself around the slap in the face of being addressed by her mother's maiden name almost in the same breath as the reference to her father, as if he were still living. Could he be? Her breath caught, but then her insides wilted. No, that had definitely been her dad in the casket those short two and half years ago. Someone was playing cruel mind games with her. Definitely someone who knew her family intimately or who had studied them minutely. Who?

"Are you ready?" Mrs. Hancock's grin faded into uncertainty.

Karissa sucked her focus back into place and forced a faint smile. "Of course."

The woman's perkiness returned full force. "Right this way."

Mrs. Hancock waved an airy hand forward as she strode in the direction of a wide, carpeted hallway. They passed several wheelchairs bearing occupants both elderly and not so elderly. Disorders like Alzheimer's disease didn't always wait to strike the aged, and accident-related brain damage could happen to anyone at any time. Considering her recent injury, Karissa could be thankful she didn't require such a facility herself.

At the rate the pair of them were moving, Karissa deduced this arrangement was not about a tour of the facility, and her guide was not an unwitting pawn of Kyle's kidnapper. Mrs. Hancock's bright smile suddenly seemed more malevolent than benevolent. Not because the wattage had changed, but because Karissa's perception had.

"In here." The woman veered through a door labeled Linen Closet.

Karissa followed—she had no choice—steeling herself for whatever she might confront. The first thing that hit her was the scent of freshly washed cotton towels. The next thing was the sharp sting of a hypodermic syringe in the side of her neck. Reflexively, Karissa struck out toward her still-smiling assailant and connected with something warm and fleshy. She couldn't be sure where her fist landed or how hard because consciousness was fading.

The world suddenly went away.

The signal from Karissa's GPS tracker showed strong on Hunter's phone as he strode as nonchalantly as he could manage toward the long, single-story building she had entered only a few moments ago. His block-and-a-half walk to the Golden Days grounds had seemed to take forever, yet had been productive. Someone had left a baseball cap on a bench at the bus stop on the corner, and he'd snatched it up and stuffed his hair under it. He would have purchased one at the strip mall where he bought the tracking lanyard, but hats were not among the goods that mall offered. Providence had provided, however. Thank you, God. His new head-covering, along with the loss of most of his wild beard, should almost make him appear to be a different person to any hostile watcher who had encountered him sometime in the past few days.

He passed through the doors into the air-conditioning. An elegantly appointed seating area presented itself in front of him. No one occupied any of the comfy-looking armchairs or the long couch, but a tall, lean man stood behind an understated reception desk to one side of the seating area.

"May I help you?" the man asked, dark eyes narrowed and suspicious.

It was maddening not to know if foe or nonthreat addressed him. For right now, he'd play the innocent card as if he were certain of the latter. He approached the desk, grin painted on his face.

"I've heard good things about this place and thought I'd pay a visit." Both halves of that statement were true, which should aid his appearance of sincerity. "Do you mind if I stroll around a bit?"

The receptionist's narrow face smoothed into warm professionalism. "We are happy to give you a tour, sir, but you must be accompanied by a staff member. Please sign in with your name and contact information while I get someone."

The man motioned to a three-ring binder open on the counter with lines and columns delineated for guests to fill out. Hunter scribbled some illegible particulars while precious seconds ticked past as the man behind the desk spoke to someone on a two-way radio.

His feet itched to race up the left-hand hallway that the tracker app indicated as Karissa's direction, but now was not the time to set off alarms of suspicion, draw security personnel and find himself evicted from the premises. Kyle was out there needing to be rescued, and both he and Karissa were willing to play out this farce with the kidnappers until the baby was recovered. However, the knowledge that Karissa could be in imminent danger was like a corkscrew digging into Hunter's heart.

How much had he already come to care for and respect this woman? Not cool, but there was nothing he could do about that unwelcome development. Once this was over, it would be best if he put plenty of distance between himself and her…provided they all survived.

At last, a smiling young woman in a colorfully patterned scrub top emerged from the right-hand hallway and introduced herself as Mandy. Beginning promotional patter, she motioned him to follow her back up the hall from which she had emerged.

Hunter stopped her with a touch on her shoulder. "Could we start in that direction?" He pointed the opposite way. "Your wall signage says the rec room is that way."

He stopped his pretext of an explanation on that note and let his guide make what she would of it.

"Sure." She shrugged and altered her course.

Hunter followed, barely restraining himself from rushing ahead. The tracker app showed Karissa's location as nearby and unmoving. His heart began to ham-

mer in his chest. Did motionless mean the worst? They
came level with the tracker indicator, and Hunter halted
while his guide continued on ahead, oblivious to his
defection.

A linen closet door stood between him and Karissa's
location. What could be going on in there? He didn't
hear a sound from inside. Hand on the knob, Hunter
gulped in a deep breath. Would he find her body on the
floor? Swiftly, he shoved the door open and let out a soft
keen at the shadowed form crumpled across the tiles.

He flipped the light switch on, and his stalled heart
suddenly jump-started. Not Karissa's body, but only
her shirt and pants, the tracker lying atop them. Hunter
snatched up the tracker's lanyard, as well as Karissa's
purse abandoned near the clothes. If Karissa's cell was
still in the handbag, it might offer valuable clues, especially if the kidnapper had sent additional texts. He
didn't have time to investigate that avenue right now,
though. He stepped back into the hallway, his gaze fran-
tically searching and cataloging the surroundings.

Residents and staff moved up and down the hallway.
Nothing suspicious or out of place. A number of the residents were in wheelchairs, either propelling themselves
or being wheeled somewhere. Some wore street clothes
and others were dressed in robes and slippers. That was
it. They had to have drugged Karissa and dressed her in
one of the generic gowns and robes. Looking like that,
they could move her anywhere around here and not be
given a second glance.

His guide for the tour had apparently noticed his ab-
sence and turned around farther up the hallway. Frowning, she was beckoning toward him to catch up with

her, but he ignored the gesture as he continued to scan
the area. His gaze settled on a woman walking briskly
toward an exit at the far end of the long hallway. She
was pushing a wheelchair, the occupant's red head lolling to one side. Karissa!

Hunter hurried up the hallway toward his tour guide,
who quickly resumed her smile, but she gave a startled yelp as he charged straight past her. The woman
with Karissa was punching a code into a panel near the
exit door. The door swung open, and Karissa's captor
wheeled her through. Hunter sped up, dodging around
gape-mouthed residents and staff. The portal was already inching shut, and if that door closed behind Karissa, he didn't have the code that would open it again.
Out in the mountain wilderness, he would have been
able to track her with good, old-fashioned woodsman's
skills. The city was a whole different story. He would
lose her trail—probably for good.

His fingertips grasped the edge of the door scant
millimeters before it would have latched shut. Ripping
with all his might against the hydraulics that wanted
to finish the closing process, he pulled the door open
and thrust his body out onto a narrow ramp sided by
cement wings that must be a loading dock.

Scant feet ahead of him, a nondescript gray van spat
exhaust fumes into his face. Karissa must have been
loaded into it, because neither the woman nor the wheelchair with its precious occupant were in sight. Sure, he
could rush in and try to attack whoever was in the van
in hopes of recovering Karissa, but he had to assume
the kidnappers were armed, and premature assault could
easily get himself or Karissa or both of them killed.

Besides, rescuing her at this time wouldn't lead them to Kyle, which was the primary point of this exercise.

The utility ladder on the back door of the van gave him a desperate idea. With fingers that seemed all thumbs, he hurriedly wrapped the lanyard of the tracker tightly around the top rung of the ladder, where it might stand some chance of going unnoticed. Then, with every ounce of willpower in him, he forced himself to step back as the vehicle accelerated out of the loading bay.

Hunter had done many difficult things in his lifetime. Standing there, fists clenching and unclenching, helplessly watching that van disappear into traffic topped the list.

TEN

Karissa gasped and sat up, gazing around a musty-smelling room dimly lit by a single lightbulb overhead. Beneath her, the cot she'd been lying on was hard and unforgiving. The walls around her were claustrophobically close. Her head throbbed, but only mildly. Apparently, the additional, unplanned rest had done her good.

She looked down at herself to find that she was clad in a robe, sock-slippers and a hospital gown, but this was no hospital. Perhaps whisking her out of some health-care facility or another, dressed as a patient, had always been the plan, but they'd been foiled at the hospital in Eugene so they'd merely changed venues—and cities. Was she still in Portland? If so, did that mean the city was her enemy's home base?

What sort of building was she in, and how had she gotten here? The last thing she remembered was perky lady sticking a needle into her neck. How much time had passed? An hour or two, a day, maybe longer? There was no clock in this room and no window that might at least reveal daylight or starlight. The cinder-block walls and cement floor suggested a storage area, possibly in a warehouse somewhere.

Did anyone friendly know where she was? Her hand flew to the spot on her breastbone where the tracker had rested. Gone, of course. Karissa's heart squeezed in upon itself. Hunter must be frantic and beating himself up, down and sideways for losing her, but it was probably best this way. At least he wouldn't be another casualty of whatever was going on.

Where was Kyle? The whole point had been to get him back—at least on Hunter's and her part. On the part of their enemy, the whole point was to get her in their clutches. The latter, at least, had worked. If only she could know Kyle was safe.

Karissa spotted a door at the other end of the room. Cautiously, she lowered her slippered feet to the cool, gritty cement floor. Her head registered only mild protest against the movement. Slowly and quietly she padded to the door panel. Holding her breath, she tried the knob and it turned. What would she find when she opened the door? A hostile party? Answers to her questions about what was going on and why? Or—she shoved the door open—a bare and empty space. The only light trickled in from a gap between another door ahead of her and the hard floor.

Cool, stale air cascaded goose bumps down Karissa's arms. She hugged herself and started to take a step farther into the dim vacantness then froze. A sound carried to her from beyond the closed door of this room where she stood. Voices. Male and coming closer. Karissa's gaze fixed on the doorknob. Would they be coming in to get her? The voices and accompanying footsteps approached quite near, but no one tried the doorknob. On mouse feet, Karissa hurried to the door panel and pressed her ear against it. Practically holding her breath, she strained to make out what was being said.

"How long until the boss gets here?" a gravelly voice asked.

"Who knows? We see him when we see him."

The voice of the second man was familiar to Karissa, and her skin crawled. A picture flashed across her mind's eye of brown eyes staring into hers while a sneer twisted a scarred mouth. Karissa's heart pounded and sweat popped out on her forehead. The man who had kidnapped her in the forest. He was still at large and a menace.

Lava erupted in Karissa's core. Her gaze scoured the room for anything that could be used as a weapon. She needed to get out of here before the mystery boss showed up. It didn't take Sherlock Holmes to deduce the big arrival could signal the end for her. Maybe she'd caused him so much trouble by now the boss wanted to be the one to do her in himself. And what about Kyle? If they still had the baby, they might be planning no good for him, either. Why was all this happening? The central question still had no answer.

Karissa returned to her tiny inner chamber and tested the metal legs on the small cot, but they were sturdy, offering no opportunity for her to dismantle one to form a makeshift club. She stripped the thin mattress from the frame. Sure enough, there were metal rods spaced periodically between the cheap springs. She pulled on each one and let out a glad cry when the last one jiggled. A little yanking back and forth broke the bar free of its weak weld. Now she had something she could use to clobber at least one guy if she could lure him in here. How she could keep the other one from shooting her while she put his partner out of commission she didn't know, but the attempt had to be made. It might be die if she did, but it would certainly be die if she didn't.

Hefting the iron bar, Karissa went to the outer door and put her ear to the door panel. The men weren't talking anymore, but a shuffle of feet and the creak of what might be a chair betrayed that at least one of them was still out there. How to get him to open the door? She could scream, but the thugs would probably just laugh at her tantrum and ignore her. Perhaps a subtler tactic would intrigue and disquiet them.

Karissa scraped her fingernails across the door panel. Whoever was outside indicated no reaction. She scratched more firmly and repeated the action over and over.

"Hey, you in there! What's up with that?" Gravel Voice hollered in agitated tones.

She heard nothing from the other guy, but that didn't mean he wasn't there. Karissa didn't speak, just continued to scratch. Her nails were wearing down and the skin on the tips of her fingers was beginning to abrade. This approach needed to yield results soon.

"All right, that's it! I'm coming in, and you better be dyin' or somethin' to be doin' that creepy scratchin'." Heavy feet stomped toward the door.

Karissa pressed her back against the wall on the hinge side of the door. She would need to let him step all the way inside with his eyes trained in front of him so she could come out from behind and clobber him.

The lock rattled, and then a burly, bald figure charged through the door. Karissa struck without hesitation and with all her might. The gun in the man's hand roared and spat, but he was already falling forward. The bullet hit the cement, spraying dislodged chunks, one of which hit Karissa's leg. She barely registered the sting as she leaped over the thug's prone body and into the outer room, prepared to launch herself at Scar Lip, but he wasn't present.

However, a different man stood there, gun pointed her direction. She skidded to a halt in front of him, iron bar raised over her head. Slowly, she lowered the bar.

"Hunter?" The word rasped from her dry throat.

He lowered his pistol and opened his arms. She rushed into them and welcomed the bear hug that wrapped her close in warmth and comfort. If only she could remain in these arms forever.

Hunter's heart swelled as he held tightly to Karissa's trembling frame. This resourceful woman took his breath away. He so very much wanted to become a permanent fixture in her life, but he'd better stop dreaming. Once the full story about him and his role in her sister's death came out, all possibility of that outcome would vanish like early morning fog beneath a summer sun. Reluctantly, he loosened his hold and gently put a small distance between them.

"Where's Kyle?" He gazed into her vivid green eyes.

"I don't know, and I'm frantic to find him."

Hunter shook his head. "I know. Me, too, but I didn't see him anywhere as I sneaked through this warehouse searching for either of you."

Karissa let out a small whimper and hung her head.

Hunter squeezed her shoulder. "We'll find bitty boy. Don't lose hope. Let me tie up the bad guys to await the cops' arrival, and then we'll get out of here."

"You called them?"

"Not yet. But I will as soon as I've got you clear. I'm not waiting around for them, because we don't know if we can trust the ones that show up."

"What about the man with the scar on his face? A minute ago, I heard him in this room talking to the one I clobbered."

A smile flickered across Hunter's lips as his gaze went past her shoulder into the room where the bald man lay sprawled, unmoving. Score another big one for the courageous Karissa.

He nodded approval at her. "Scar Lip is in the outer hallway taking a nap similar to your guy's. I put him out of commission with the butt of my pistol as he exited the room and then I stepped in here in time to see you take care of the other hired thug."

An answering smile trembled on Karissa's lips. "I don't know how to thank you. How did you find me? That woman at Golden Days must have removed my tracker when she put me in this ridiculous gown."

"Let's just say I was close enough behind you to get the tracker onto the vehicle that took off with you inside."

"Thank You, Jesus." Karissa slumped.

Hunter reached out to steady her, but she'd already pulled herself together and squared her shoulders.

"We need to get out of here quickly," she said. "I overheard the goons saying that *he*, the big boss, was due here any time. We don't know how much muscle he will bring with him."

"At least now we know the gender of the person we're pitted against," Hunter said.

"Narrows the suspect pool considerably."

He grinned at the dry humor in her voice as he scanned the sparsely furnished area for something that would serve as restraints for the thugs who had been guarding Karissa. A battered metal desk held the remnants of a card game the guards must have been playing. A single lamp with an extension cord perched on the edge of the desk. The cord would have to do.

With Karissa's help, he dragged the scar-lipped thug over to his buddy in the outer room of the makeshift cell where Karissa had been held and bound them tightly together. He scooped up the bald thug's gun and tucked it in his own waistband, along with the firearm he'd taken from Scar Lip and the one he'd borrowed from Buck's friend. Quite an arsenal he'd accrued. Then he shut the door and locked it with the key that was still in the hole.

From the front of the building, a sound reached them—a door opening and closing.

A tremor ran through Hunter. "Someone's coming."

Grasping Karissa's upper arm, he jerked his head toward a side door in the room her guards had occupied. Hopefully, that direction might lead them to a rear exit of the warehouse. Sure enough, they entered a corridor with the option to head toward the back of the building. Ushering Karissa ahead of him, Hunter drew the Ruger from his waistband and kept one eye on their rear as they moved almost noiselessly but not nearly as quickly as he would like.

God, please help us to find an exit soon.

Natural sunlight beckoned from a window up ahead, and a shout from behind notified them that the unconscious thugs had been found. Pursuit was about to begin. More shouts and angry voices alerted them that they had multiple adversaries.

Without being told, Karissa increased her speed, and Hunter stayed on her tail. They reached the wall with the window, and there the corridor turned to the left into a tiny foyer framing a metal exit door. Hunter expelled a breath he hadn't known he was holding. He stepped in front of Karissa and rammed sideways into the bar latch. A raucous alarm sounded as the door sprang open, admitting late afternoon sunlight and fresh air. Hunter scanned the asphalt parking area, his gun following his gaze. So far, so good. No vehicles or people in sight. Just the wall of another warehouse several dozen feet distant.

"C'mon." He motioned Karissa to precede him. "Your car keys were in your purse that got left at Golden Days Care Center, so I grabbed your Toyota to follow you. It's parked in the alley one building over. We need to make a run for it. Keep me between you and whoever is after us."

She nodded and scurried ahead. Hunter trotted after her. If only he'd had some way to secure that door they'd just come through. As it was, his body as a shield and the firepower at his disposal were all that stood between Karissa and the determined killers coming after them. It was possible that one of them was the mastermind behind all this mayhem, but they couldn't afford to pause in their flight to get eyes on the guy.

They reached the second warehouse that offered a

modicum of cover and skirted the wall toward the alleyway. A loud bark sounded, and a bullet pinged off the brick a few inches from Hunter's head. They had a shooter coming up behind them. He whirled and returned fire. The gunman ducked back around the corner of the warehouse.

Ahead of him, Karissa broke into a dead run. Hunter followed suit, even as he fired another shot toward the lurking thug to discourage him from popping out again and firing on them with better results than the first time. They reached the end of the warehouse and the beginning of the alley. Hunter grabbed Karissa's shoulder and halted her flight. He peered around the corner of the building. Her little car sat, quiet and unattended by enemy goons. Probably they hadn't been able to locate it yet.

"Time to skedaddle," he told Karissa.

"I'll drive. You shoot."

She held out her hand for her car keys. Hunter plunked them into her palm. Then he sent another shot behind them toward the guy who was starting to poke his head around the building again. Shouts from other directions let them know their pursuers were attempting to close in around them.

"Go!" he rasped urgently.

Karissa went, her slipper-clad feet fairly skimming the pavement. Hunter's hiking boots pounded after her. From the corner of a building ahead, an assailant jumped out, but Hunter pulled the trigger and sent him leaping backward into cover. Out of the corner of his eye, Hunter made out Karissa reaching the Toyota and lunging into place behind the wheel. Hunter hopped in beside her and hit the button to roll down the window even as she started the car and floored the gas.

The little vehicle showed enough get-up-and-go to thrust them back against their seats. They roared out of the alley. A loud crash announced that the rear window had succumbed to a bullet. Hunter answered fire, though whether he hit anyone he couldn't tell. However, getting away was the point. Shooting someone wasn't—as much as he felt like taking these goons down, especially Mr. Mastermind. Hunter scanned their surroundings and saw no sign of pursuit. Yet, anyway.

"Where to?" Karissa demanded as they left her captors in the rearview mirror. "My apartment is here in Portland, but I'm sure that's not a wise or safe place to go."

"Yes, someplace safe is an urgent need right now. Just drive as far away from here as you can get while I give the matter some thought. But first, a call to the police."

Hunter got out his phone and, without giving his identity or mentioning Karissa, he made a 911 call, though he surmised that the gunfire in the area had already drawn their attention.

"I have an idea," he said, pocketing his phone. "If you'll trust me with something weird."

"If? You've been my lifeline." Karissa sent him a sidelong look as she continued to barrel down streets that were taking on a more and more residential quality.

"Best slow down," he advised. "We don't need to get stopped by a traffic cop."

She complied by easing back her foot on the gas pedal. "Like I said. Where to? Another biker bar?"

"Quite the opposite. I know a guy in Portland who makes the Fortune 500 list and has promised me a favor."

"Let me guess. You saved his cat from a fire."

The strain in her tone let Hunter know she was bravely battling terror with corny humor.

He grinned. "It was his dog, actually, when his pool house burned down."

Karissa shot him a sharp look. "You're kidding, right?"

"Nope. He said if he could ever do something for me, just ask. Under normal circumstances I wouldn't dream of taking him up on that offer. Unprofessional to the max, but right now, I don't care about professional ethics. Besides which, I'm not a firefighter anymore, so I don't have that particular ethic to violate. Nobody, but nobody will look for you with him. In fact, his house is so big it might take anybody a week to locate you in there."

Karissa spurted a chuckle. "If I'm hiding out, what are you going to do?"

"Dig for clues, so you may have to let me pick your brain in possibly painful areas."

She let out a soft hum. "Whatever brain I have functional you may pick, but I don't like the idea of you out there sleuthing alone."

"Would you rather draw major attention by appearing in public in that getup?" He motioned toward her robe and slippers.

Karissa's silence answered Hunter.

"Even from hiding," he continued, "you can always

get online and find out anything in your family's digital footprint that might tell you about potential enemies."

She sat up straighter. "Yes, I can do that. Here, let me pull over and give you the driver's seat, so you can take me to your rich guy's palatial mansion. Though what he'll think about you showing up with a woman dressed like a hospital patient I shudder to speculate."

They stopped and switched places in the front seat.

"Great! Here's my purse," she said as she pulled the object onto her lap from the floor of the passenger side. "I could start the search on my cell while you're driving."

Karissa dug out the phone and started pecking away. The cell dinged with a message then another and another. Hunter glanced her way and met her wide-eyed gaze.

"I'm afraid to look." Her voice quivered.

"No need to be afraid," he said, reaching over and giving her hand a quick squeeze. "I'm here."

Karissa swiped then gasped and stared at the screen. She swiped and stared again, a strangled cry leaving her throat.

"You didn't tell me!" she cried. "You said you were there, but you didn't let on that you were at fault. Why didn't you tell me?"

The blood turned to icy sludge in Hunter's veins. *No! Not now!*

"These texts are all links to news articles like this." She thrust her phone toward him.

Hunter didn't need to look, but he glanced anyway. His sober, smoke-smudged face—clean shaven and scar-free—stared back at him from an unflattering photo taken of him at a fire prior to the one that claimed Anissa. Karissa's twin's pretty face appeared next to his. The headline bathed him in hot shame.

"'Is Firefighter Negligence to Blame for Fatality in House Fire?'"

Hunter opened his mouth to attempt some explanation. But what explanation? It was too late for that, anyway. He clamped his jaw shut. The contempt in Karissa's eyes flayed him alive.

ELEVEN

Blackness edged Karissa's vision. She could scarcely draw oxygen into her lungs, and a giant, invisible fist squeezed her heart. Anissa was dead because of this man next to her. The guy was no hero. His taking up of her cause had to be nothing more than an attempt to soothe his guilt. Or was he actually part of this whole plot? No, she couldn't make sense of that conclusion when he'd had more than ample opportunity to either do away with her himself or hand her over to whoever was trying to kill her. The minutes-ago gunfight was a case in point.

"Don't you see what our enemy is trying to do?" Hunter's desperate tones reached her as if from a distance. "He's trying to get you to hate me and reject my protection so I'll be out of his way."

"At this moment, I don't much care." Her words came out high and thin. "I can hardly bear to sit next to you."

Her glance at him revealed a stony profile leached of color.

"I understand your reaction, and I respect it," he said softly, but with steel undergirding his tone. "However, for the next few minutes, anyway, you'll have to endure my presence. After I drop you off with my guy, you don't have to see me again—provided we can get to the bottom of what is going on, find Kyle and secure your safety."

"*Right.* Then you can ride off into the sunset with the score evened up, and you don't have to carry your guilt anymore."

"It doesn't work that way, Karissa. We both know there is one answer for guilt and shame, and good deeds don't make up for or earn anything."

She sniffed, deliberately staring out the side window and tamping down the nudge in her gut that this man spoke the truth—that he was, in fact, a brother in the Lord, regardless of his colossal failure toward her family, and that, as a Christian, she was supposed to forgive. Just like Jesus forgave his tormenters from the cross. Nothing so charitable was in her mind or heart right now.

What was the matter with her that she had felt attraction to this man? That she had to fight its insidious pull even now? What a betrayal of her love for her sister! How could she bear to so much as look at Hunter one minute more? Anissa was *dead* because this guy didn't do his job! She shook with the blaze roaring through her.

Karissa sat in silence, fists clenched, while Hunter called the man whose home he wanted to use as a safe house. Turned out the guy was off globe-trotting somewhere, but he said he'd call his housekeeper to let them in. The woman, he'd told Hunter, would be around for at least another hour before she went home for the day.

Karissa acknowledged this information with a small grunt—the most she could manage without spewing more venom in Hunter's direction.

Soon, their journey took them uphill into the Arlington Heights district, a posh residential area overlooking the city. The view was truly breathtaking, but her breath was already taken by the information she'd received about Hunter. To think she'd admired and trusted him…even nurtured hope that they could explore the possibilities of an ongoing relationship when—if—this mess got sorted out and they were both still alive.

Dusk was starting to creep around them when they drove under a vine-covered archway onto a horseshoe driveway with a massive two-story home at its curved apex. Multiple dormers peered out upon a spacious lawn and garden layout that rioted color in neatly manicured formations. This much real estate in this upscale neighborhood was pricey indeed.

Without a glance in her direction, Hunter exited the car and strode up to the front door. On feet that felt as if they were moving through sludge, Karissa followed. Her head was pounding unbearably again. This entire day had brimmed with the kind of stress the doctor had warned her against, but she hadn't had much control over how any of it unfolded. She could only thank God that, once again, she was delivered from the clutches of a murderer. A whisper in her soul reminded her that God had wrought this deliverance in large part through the damaged ex-fireman who now stood at the door of the mansion arranging for her safekeeping.

She shushed the whisper and trudged on faltering legs up the steps to the front door. A matronly woman with her salt-and-pepper hair arranged into a severe bun motioned her to come inside. As Karissa stepped over the threshold, her head started to spin and her knees to buckle. A masculine exclamation was followed by strong arms coming around her. Consciousness faded to nothingness.

In the deepening darkness, Hunter guided Karissa's Toyota toward Portland Fire and Rescue Station Number 1. Leaving Karissa in Mrs. Peterson's care had been gut-wrenching, but also necessary. The housekeeper seemed more than competent. She'd assured him she'd look in on Karissa before she left for the night. He'd offered to pay her to stay over, but the woman needed to be at a granddaughter's choir concert that evening and refused his offer. Naturally, the housekeeper's departure meant Karissa would be in the house alone until Hunter accomplished his mission. He wasn't exactly comfortable with that idea, but a better option hadn't presented itself. He'd have to make sure he got back to her side as quickly as possible—whether she wanted him there or not.

Also, Karissa losing consciousness was worrisome, but the intern at the hospital had warned that she could do so at any time if she left medical care too soon, especially if she underwent stress. Considering the day they'd had, it was a marvel Karissa hadn't passed out sooner. When he'd left, she was resting comfortably, her pulse and respirations were normal, and her pupil dilation was uniform—all good signs that she just needed time to take it easy and recover.

No, Hunter had to let go of his worries about Karissa's

care and concentrate on exposing who wanted to harm her, as well as whatever he could uncover regarding Kyle's whereabouts. In that regard, a new approach had suddenly occurred to him. One that might not have swum into his consciousness had their enemy not chosen suddenly to turn the spotlight on Hunter's supposed culpability in Anissa's fiery death. If, as Karissa and he had tentatively concluded, the deaths in Karissa's family were all orchestrated and not accidents at all, that meant someone may have sabotaged the equipment that failed during the tragic fire, and the same person could well have disposed of the checklist that would have proven Hunter had done the safety check after all.

Had he been framed as part of this major conspiracy? Hope leaped in him at the thought. Yet the idea would seem ludicrous, except for the fact that the ferocity of the attacks on Karissa these past few days demonstrated a will of extraordinary resourcefulness and determination. Had this mastermind bribed or coerced one of Hunter's fellow firefighters at the station to do his dirty work? If anyone had acted as a saboteur, it had to be someone with access to restricted areas in the fire station and intimate familiarity with the equipment. Only another firefighter fit that bill.

The idea curdled Hunter's stomach. In their line of work, his colleagues had become more like brothers and sisters than coworkers. For one to betray another—betray the very calling of their life's work—was nearly unthinkable. Yet there was a possibility that it had happened. Now, it was up to Hunter to expose the traitor, not only for the sake of proving his own innocence— that was a peripheral issue at the moment—but as a tangible link to whoever was behind the vendetta against the Landon family.

Conflicting emotions rioting within him, Hunter pulled the Toyota into a parking spot a block from the large, rectangular redbrick building that housed Station 1 in Old Town. The bottom floor where the trucks, engines and vans were housed was dark. Some of the windows for offices and living quarters on the second and third floors glowed with golden warmth. At all times, a full duty crew occupied the building, composed of a deputy chief, three company officers, three firefighter paramedics and six firefighters. The crews were trained and certified in a gamut of technical rescue disciplines, including rescues from heights and depths, confined spaces, collapsed structures, and vehicle and machinery extraction. They could even perform dive rescues during amphibious emergencies. For now, all seemed quiet in the neighborhood this station served. That status could, and inevitably would, change in a heartbeat.

Living in the constantly alert tension between action and calm, the crew would be doing homey things like cooking and cleaning, maybe playing cards in raucous fellowship. A dull pain ached in Hunter's chest. This had been his home away from home for many years. He'd been in line to eventually take a deputy chief slot, but unproven suspicion of negligence undid everything for which he'd worked and trained.

Every man and woman in there considered "safety first" a chief tenet and saving lives a prime directive. Their motto was Always Ready, Always There. Deliberately sabotaging safety was the lowest any crew member could go. Hunter couldn't imagine any of his colleagues doing so, but he was going in there prepared to rip the mask off the culprit and, hopefully, that person could be induced to expose the murderous mastermind. God was going to have to orchestrate how this unmasking played out, because he had no time for subtlety or finesse, just a full-frontal charge and hope that the shock would shake something—no, someone—loose.

Hunter opened the door of the Toyota and stepped out into the muggy dark of a Portland summer night. His heavy hiking boots beat a steady tattoo on the pavement, carrying him stride by stride into a confrontation he dreaded as much as he welcomed this chance to know—really know—what had happened. He'd seen the way his crew looked at him after the tragedy. The suspicion and uneasiness that had replaced trust and comradery hurt him as much or more than his burns ever had, and in his shame, he had received their condemnation as his just due. Hunter had no reason to believe his former colleagues would view him any differently this night, but he was going to face them, look each one in the eyes and find the gaze that turned away.

Blood pumping hard enough to send faint throbs through his healing arm wound, he arrived at the station house door and mashed his thumb on the doorbell.

Karissa came to with a start. What had awakened her? No apparent reason presented itself. Maybe she'd simply gotten enough sleep. Her environment was dark and quiet and smelled soothingly of lavender. Where was she?

Then she remembered arriving at some rich guy's house in Portland's Arlington Heights district. She must have passed out and, judging by the softness of the mattress and pillow beneath her, been carried to bed. No doubt Hunter had done the carrying. The thought both comforted and repelled her. She should feel utter disgust, yet a piece of her wished he were nearby. Maybe he was somewhere in this house, or had he left her to go sleuthing as he'd proposed? Knowing Hunter, the answer was the latter. The guy did what he said he was going to do. A lot of people in this world could take lessons from his faithfulness. These traits flew in the face of his presumed negligence in the fire that took her sister and wounded Hunter, but what was she to think? What should she believe? Trusting Hunter now seemed like a betrayal of her sister, and yet, Hunter had wormed his way into her heart, and it was going to take more than willpower to dig him out again.

With great deliberation and effort, she shoved thoughts of the ex-firefighter away. He didn't deserve her attention, and she didn't have time to deal with the conflicting emotions thoughts of him aroused.

Karissa sat up cautiously, testing her brain's reaction to the movement. Nothing. Not a twinge of pain. Maybe she would quit passing out at unexpected moments.

A digital clock on the bedside table told her it was nearing 10:00 p.m. She couldn't have been sleeping more than a couple of hours. In the glow of the clock's numbers, she made out the shape of a lamp. She reached over and flicked on the light. The bedroom she occupied was spacious, as was the ornate four-poster bed with ruffled canopy. Judging by the decor featuring ballerinas and princesses, this room was made for a young girl. An ornately framed photo next to the clock featured a sweet-faced child, probably still single digits of age, with sparkling blue eyes and blond pigtails. The owner of the space? Had Karissa displaced her? Or, more likely, the girl was traveling with the man who owned the house. Maybe the whole family was on the journey.

If Hunter wasn't in the house, maybe the housekeeper had stayed behind, but if she had gone home, then Karissa could well be alone in this enormous place. Her heart rate sped up at the thought of her lonely vulnerability. Her only comfort was the belief that her enemies couldn't possibly know her whereabouts.

Karissa swung her feet onto the floor, and her toes touched soft carpeting. She found herself looking straight into a mirror attached to a dainty dressing table. The reflection showed her bright hair tumbling in disarray around her shoulders. At least her cheeks had a little color, and her eyes looked alert. Wide-awake, in fact. She badly needed a shower, though. Possibly the open doorway next to the dressing table led to a bathroom. But if she grabbed a shower, what would she dress in afterward? This hospital gown needed to go.

She stepped to the doorway and flicked on the light. Yes, a bathroom. And better yet, fluffy towels were laid out on the marble vanity top, along with a set of clothing—leggings and a long-tailed shirt with accompanying undergarments, as well as a pair of flip-flops that look as if they would fit her. This housekeeper was nothing if not accommodating. Karissa didn't waste another moment availing herself of the invitation to feel clean and decently dressed again.

* * *

In the moonlit dark of the massive first floor garage of Portland Fire Station 1, Hunter waited, inhaling familiar odors of diesel fuel and residual smoke that clung to the equipment. A half hour ago, he'd been chatting up his former firefighter friends in the living area upstairs, pretending like crazy that he wasn't affected by the reserve of his ex-comrades or the stilted nature of the conversation. With casual care, he'd dropped hints that he was going to pressure the powers that be to look more closely into his case. He wasn't satisfied with this inconclusive limbo. All of his former buddies had seemed uncomfortable with that idea, but one guy—Ethan Crenshaw, a rookie at the time of Anissa's fatal house fire—went pale and stuck out his chin like he was angry, the kind of anger that was fed by the fear that lurked behind his eyes.

Then Hunter had left the station—or pretended to leave. A pair of his former comrades had escorted him to the door and let him out. He pretended to walk away, but as soon as he'd heard footsteps retreating from the doorway, he'd turned back quickly and grabbed the door in the nick of time before it could shut and latch, locking him out. Now, he waited between a hose-laden fire engine and a ladder truck. Soon, the lights in the stairwell leading up to the living quarters winked out. Sack time for the duty crew. In their line of work, sleep was a precious commodity.

Slightly less than ten minutes later, Hunter made out a shadowy figure creeping down the stairs. The man reached the bottom step and tiptoed past a small window, exposing his face in a stream of light from the street. Ethan, all right. Then the guy stepped deeper into the darkness. Hunter soft-footed closer then ducked behind an EMT truck as Ethan awakened his phone and tapped in a number. Hunter activated the record feature on his own cell in his pants pocket.

"Raines was here!" Hunter's quarry whisper-rasped into the phone then paused to receive what must have been a sharp response, because the guy jerked as if struck. "I don't care if you told me not to call you. He showed up, and I'm telling you, he knows something's hinky." Then Crenshaw's shoulders relaxed. "All right, you take care of it, then, because if I go down for this, you will, too." More muffled but sharp words from the other end sent the guy's free hand into the air in a gesture of surrender. "I'm not threatening you, man. Just stating a fact."

Crenshaw ended the call and turned straight into Hunter's chest as he stepped out from behind cover.

Quick as a cobra, Hunter snatched the phone from the other man's hand and pocketed it. "Who were you talking to?"

For answer, Crenshaw backpedaled and grabbed up a tire iron lying on the bumper of nearby truck. The man took a vicious swipe at Hunter's head. He ducked sideways barely in time for the attack to whistle past his ear. The iron hit the rear of the truck with a loud *clang*. Ethan pursued Hunter in a mad frenzy of blows that he avoided only by keeping his cool and bobbing and weaving. If his opponent started frothing at the mouth, Hunter wouldn't be surprised. The guy was fighting on the adrenaline rush of sheer panic and creating a ruckus of dented metal and smashed glass.

Very soon alarmed shouts and running feet sounded overhead and then descended the stairs toward the combatants. Hunter kept his attention on that viciously swinging iron and at last spotted his chance when the tool buried itself in the side of a pumper truck. He rammed his shoulder into Crenshaw, breaking the man's hold on his deadly weapon. Then he followed up with a jab into his assailant's kidney that doubled him over. Hunter's other fist delivered an uppercut to Crenshaw's jaw, and the man collapsed and lay retching on the cement.

"What's going on down here?" Deputy Chief James strode forward.

"Here's the guy who sabotaged the equipment during the fatal fire where I was injured." Hunter jabbed a finger toward his downed opponent.

"Don't believe him," Crenshaw wailed and followed up with curses.

"Shut up," James barked. "You going after Hunter with a tire iron doesn't look too great for you." The captain returned his attention to Hunter. "What proof do you have?"

He pulled out his phone and played the conversation he'd recorded. Context and tone made the meaning abundantly clear. The eyes of Hunter's former comrades that had so recently gazed at him with suspicion now glared daggers at the man cowering on the floor.

"Who paid you to betray your entire code of honor?" Hunter demanded.

"Not money." Crenshaw denied and sat up, hugging his knees to his chest and rocking back and forth. "He threatened my family."

"Who?" Hunter and James demanded simultaneously.

"I don't know." Crenshaw sniffled, utterly broken. "I only dealt with a go-between."

A slow burn crept through every atom of Hunter's body. Over the past two years, he had endured the torture of recovery from his injuries, as well as the panic attacks and torment of a conscience that never rested. He'd left his life's work and buried himself in the backwoods as a form of defense against his shame. Shame that he now discovered had never been his to begin with. Even worse, the awful truth was confirmed: Karissa had lost her twin sister—not simply to a tragic, accidental fire—but to deliberate and diabolical murder.

Hunter pulled Crenshaw's phone from his pocket and accessed the call log. The last number his traitorous colleague had called was unfamiliar to Hunter. He handed the phone to the deputy chief.

"I've got to go. I left someone alone who needs protecting, and I need to get back to her. I'm trusting you to contact law enforcement and find out whose number this is."

"Consider it done." James nodded.

"I'll send you a copy of the recording, too." Hunter turned on his heel and charged for the door.

"Go get 'em, Raines!" a former colleague's cry chased him, followed by a raucous cheer from multiple voices.

If Hunter's mind had been at ease about Karissa and Kyle, the moment would have been one of deep satisfaction. Later—if there was a later for him—he would let the healing balm in. Right now, he wanted—no, needed—to rejoin Karissa and give her the news that he was *not* to blame for her sister's death.

Losing that beautiful, admirable woman's respect and trust had felt like death to his soul. He was desperate for her to look at him again like he was a man she might consider more than a friend. Despite the dire circumstances, they'd been looking at each other like that for some time now, and he'd been resisting the attraction with everything in him because of the way he thought he'd failed her family. Now everything was different. Potent with possibilities. They just needed to find Kyle and put a stop to whoever was trying to kill Karissa. Tall orders, for sure, but at this moment he was feeling ten feet tall.

Thirty seconds flat found him gunning the Toyota as fast as he dared without attracting police attention. A stop for a speeding ticket was not an option. He whizzed toward a green light without slowing down. As he entered the intersection, a dump truck with darkened headlamps charged through the red light and bore down on him, going for the T-bone. A familiar tactic, but potentially deadly, and it was too late for evasive action.

TWELVE

Hair wet but brushed out, Karissa padded on bare feet, carrying the flip-flops, down an ornate, curved staircase and into a formal living room. Turning on lights as she went, she made her way deeper into the house until she reached a state-of-the-art kitchen. She'd done a sweep of the upstairs bedrooms to see if Hunter was sleeping in one of them, but all the rooms were empty. Thus far, she hadn't run into a living soul. The housekeeper must have left for the day.

Karissa's stomach growled at sight of a plate of chocolate chip cookies laid out invitingly on the counter next to a familiar object—her purse. Grabbing the bag with one hand and a cookie with the other, Karissa hopped onto a stool at the island counter. As she munched the cookie, she dug around in the purse for her cell phone, but it didn't seem to be there. Frowning, she scanned the area and spotted the phone on a nearby counter, holding down a white sheet of paper folded in half. A note from Hunter, no doubt.

Licking cookie crumbs off her fingers, she tugged the note free of the phone and unfolded it. *Ms. Landon,* it began. Clearly not a communication from Hunter. Must be from the housekeeper.

Chills pebbled her flesh as she read the rest of the block-lettered message.

You want answers, and I have decided that your resourcefulness has earned them. Besides, this cat-and-mouse back-and-forth has gotten to be rather fun. Shall we begin a scavenger hunt? Continue to display such ingenuity, and your reward at the end shall be Kyle. I may even decide to let him live. However, I cannot extend you the same courtesy or my purpose would be utterly thwarted. You will find your first clue in the study, but you will need humility to find it. I'm sure you understand the ground rules include no law enforcement involvement.

PS: By the time you discover this note, it will already be too late for the firefighter.

Deep in her core, a soundless wail erupted. This horrible man couldn't have gotten to Hunter. He couldn't be gone. She wouldn't believe it. She couldn't bear it. Yet, why did she care so much about the survival of a man who had so horribly failed her sister? She couldn't entirely shake the niggling suspicion that he had deceived her into thinking he was an ally when he was actually an opportunist bent on helping her to assuage his guilt over her sister's death? Yet, a still, small voice in her core rebelled at the assumption of his culpability. Was she that far gone in her unacknowledged feelings for

Hunter that she'd choose him over loyalty to Anissa's memory? She couldn't afford to think like this.

As she pushed unfruitful speculations about Hunter away, another thought chilled her core. What if she wasn't alone in the house after all? What if whoever left this note was lurking around, waiting to pounce and kill her? Goose bumps pebbled her skin. She sat still, straining her ears for sounds that could only be made by human presence, but only caught the tick-tick-tick of the clock in the kitchen. Releasing a pent-up breath, she shook her head. Imagination was running away with her. If the person who left the note had been sent to kill her, she'd be dead right now. He would have found her conveniently sound asleep, dispatched her, and that would have been the end of it. Apparently her enemy had decided to torment her further before ending her life.

Right now, her task was to find the study and locate the clue. She left the kitchen by another doorway and found herself in a long hall at the end of which appeared to be a massive front door, the one through which she'd entered the house. Padding up the hallway, she came to an open great room on one side. On the other side, a pair of French doors led into a spacious area furnished in masculine style with a large, leather-topped desk, an enormous fireplace, wall-to-wall shelves of books and office-type equipment. The study, for sure.

She began to step into the room when a noise at the front door froze her in place. Who was there? Pulse rate rocketing, she stared around wildly for some type of weapon to defend herself. *There!* The fireplace poker. She ran into the room and grabbed it. Hefting the object, she crept out of the study toward the front door. The knob rattled as someone strained to turn it, but the locking mechanism resisted. Apparently, the person on the doorstep wasn't someone who had a key. An enemy? Far too likely. Standing to the side of the entry, Karissa lifted the poker high and waited.

A knock sounded, and then a voice called her name. The strength ebbed from her arm, and it fell limp to her side. The poker left nerveless fingers and clattered to the tile floor. As if the noise were a spur to the intruder, a heavy body rammed against the door panel. The whole frame shivered.

Karissa found her voice even as she unlocked the door. "It's okay, Hunter. I'm fine."

The door opened and he surged inside, filling Karissa's world. Strong arms wrapped her close, and she didn't resist. How could she when her knees were gelatin, incapable of holding her up?

Hunter's warm breath teased the hairs on the top of her head. "I didn't do it, Karissa. I'm innocent. Someone else sabotaged the equipment. Your sister was murdered, but I had nothing to do with it."

"What?" She looked up into his face and gasped. His bottom lip was cut and swollen, an eye was puffy, thin cuts raked red lines across one cheek, and bloodstains marred his shirt.

"You're hurt."

"Just a little skirmish with a dump truck. I'm okay, but your car is toast. After the truck rammed me, the guys inside it started using me for target practice, but then sirens began closing in, so they skedaddled. I ran away and grabbed a taxi before the cops could arrive and demand a statement."

"You found out who sabotaged the fire rescue equipment?"

"One of my colleagues. Our mutual enemy threatened his family if he didn't do it. I'm so sorry."

Breath coming in shallow puffs, Karissa reached up and brushed her fingertips across the scars edging his eye. Her insides expanded as big as all outdoors. What a relief in the midst of danger looming all around. Hunter was innocent! The words rang through her soul like joyous bells. What did that say about her feelings for this man? Too bad there was no time to explore the possibilities. In fact, that time might never come if her enemy had his way.

"You were as much a victim as my sister," she told him in choked tones. "You were nearly killed trying to save her with faulty equipment. I can't even imagine how much you've suffered. Something inside me knew you couldn't be guilty. Not when you've demonstrated nothing but courage and reliability and faithfulness. That's your nature—your character. *I'm* the one who's sorry."

"Don't be." He hugged her close again, and she wrapped her arms around him. "You have no idea how thankful I am that God brought you into my life—not just because our meeting produced an opportunity to clear my name, but because I've had the privilege of meeting *such an amazing person as you*." He drew back from their embrace, and she looked into his intense gray gaze. "No matter what happens," he said, "I'll always be grateful for that unexpected and undeserved blessing."

She nodded, eyes clouding with tears. "I feel the same way, but Hunter, Kyle is still missing, and I received this." She showed him the written note.

His brows knotted as he read it. "Somehow, our mutual enemy not only found you here at this unpredictable location, but someone in his employ was able to gain access to the house in order to leave this note. I'm guessing the guy does have some sort of tracker on you among your belongings. It could be something on your phone that we don't have the expertise to detect, or it could be in the lining of your purse, but that scarcely matters now. We have to follow his scavenger hunt clues. But remember this—" he laid his warm palm against her cheek "—the guy was wrong about me being eliminated. And now his minion at the fire department has been exposed. I'm predicting that his plan is starting to unravel."

"I pray you're right, but we still need to find that scavenger hunt clue right here in the study." She waved toward the expensively decorated office.

Every nerve within her stretched to the breaking point as they searched through the room high and low. Would either of them even recognize this clue if they saw it? A half hour later, they had found nothing resembling a clue to Kyle's whereabouts. Her stomach twisted in knots.

With a baby's life at stake, they'd shamelessly snooped through everything except the locked drawer in the desk and the safe Hunter discovered behind a painting on the wall above the fireplace. They had no key to open the former or combination to open the latter. Surely, their mastermind wouldn't leave the clue in a spot they couldn't access.

Karissa performed a 360-degree scan of the entire room. Nothing. With a sob, she plopped in a heap on the cushy carpeting. Was this part of the game? Telling them there was a clue when there wasn't one?

Hunter stepped over and sat down beside her, cross-legged. She leaned her head against his shoulder, inhaling his masculine, woodsy odor.

"Hang in there," he said, but his tone was thin and stressed.

"How? I've been praying for wisdom, praying for Kyle, praying for us. Is God even listening?"

Lifting her head, she wiped hot tears from her cheeks and dried her eyes with her shirt. Bitterness coated her tongue—the taste of defeat.

She gripped the edge of the desk to help haul herself to her feet, and her thumb brushed across a slick substance that wasn't desk varnish. With an indrawn breath, she canted her head to check out the anomaly. A small photograph was taped to the underside of the desk's lip. Hadn't the note said she'd need to be humble to find the clue? Well, here it was, and she'd had to access it from a position on the floor.

A squeal left Karissa's lips as she pulled the photo free of the desk. "Here it is. But what is it?"

She lifted the photo, and they both stared down at Kyle's smiling baby face. The little boy was strapped into a car seat that had been placed directly beside a familiar Portland landmark—one of the two ornate towers that guarded both ends of the drawbridge portion of Burnside Bridge spanning the Willamette River. The picture was taken at night—surely this very night—but the spot was bathed in headlights that sparkled on the water in the background of the shot. A big letter *E* was drawn in permanent marker on the tower.

"I guess we're headed for the east tower," Hunter said.

"I'm surprised they cared enough to put him in a car seat." Karissa sniffed. "How are we going to get there?"

"I'll call a taxi."

"Let me grab my phone and my purse."

"Leave them behind."

"But what if one of our upcoming clues involves cell phone communication?"

"Give the guy credit for more creativity than that. I refuse to be tracked any longer."

Karissa shrugged. "No matter, I guess. We're on a scavenger hunt being led by these creeps. They're going to know where we are regardless."

The wait for the taxi seemed like forever, and the ride to Burnside Bridge began in tense silence. If worry were a sodden blanket, they were both wrapped in it. Traffic was light, and soon they neared the bridge.

"I remember now!" Karissa exclaimed.

Hunter whipped his head toward her. "Remember what?"

"I've been racking my brains as to why our enemy might send us to this particular spot. He doesn't seem to do anything at random."

The taxi slid to a stop near the east tower, but Karissa made no move to get out, and Hunter stayed put with her.

"A few years back," she said, "this was the scene of

a horrible tragedy. A businessman gone bust ran his car off the bridge near here with his wife and young son in the car. They were all killed. Do you suppose that event is somehow connected to the vendetta against us?"

"You may be onto something. It fits with this guy's devious mind to give us a clue as to his motive within a clue to Kyle's whereabouts. We should do some research and—"

"Hey, you two, are you getting out?" the taxi driver interrupted in grumpy tones. "I'm sitting in a driving lane, and a cop could come along and ticket me at any time."

"Oh, sure." Hunter handed the driver his fare and tip in cash he'd gotten from an ATM when he was out and about acquiring a cell phone and a gun. "Come on."

He motioned to Karissa, and they got out. Then they watched the taxi's headlights fade away.

Karissa shrugged. "Now we're without wheels."

"We can always call for another taxi. Let's find that next clue."

"I think it's sitting right in front of us." Karissa pointed to a skateboard perched in the spot where Kyle's car seat had been in the photograph.

Hunter grunted. "Good eye. Guess we hoof it to the skate park under the bridge." He snatched up the board and headed up the sidewalk.

Karissa fell into step beside Hunter. She hugged herself as she put forth the effort to match his determined stride. The summer night was warm, but the breeze off the water had a cool touch against her skin. A shiver coursed through her. What were they doing, following the instructions of a devious and deadly mind? Yet, what else could they do when a baby's fate hung in the balance? To be honest with herself, she couldn't see a positive ending to this scenario.

"Do you still have your gun?" Karissa asked her companion.

"Yes."

"If—no, *when* we find Kyle, please don't use it anywhere near him."

"Trust me."

She did. With every molecule of her being.

They soon arrived at the iconic Burnside Skatepark that had been featured in movies and documentaries, as well as a number of skateboarding computer games. The park was still in use, but past its heyday, and the site was eerie, dark and deserted. The place smelled of metal shavings and human sweat—odors the concrete had absorbed from skateboard wheels and the people who rode them.

"Have you ever skated here?" Karissa asked out of pure nervousness, not really expecting an affirmative answer.

"I love this place," Hunter said. "When I was a teenager, Burnside Skatepark was my home away from home. But then, I grew up in this rough area of Portland, so some of the more sketchy clientele didn't scare me, and the visitors from around the world fascinated me. Actually, I think this place kept a lot of us kids out of trouble."

He turned on the flashlight feature of his cell phone. Karissa let out a little squeak as the beam hit her eyes. "Oops, sorry," he said, turning the beam toward himself, illuminating his upper body and part of a deep skate bowl directly behind him. A shot rang out. Hunter fell backward without a sound, and his body disappeared into the bowl. Karissa began to scream, but a large hand clamped over her mouth. All that escaped was a shriek from her heart.

Hunter hit the bottom of the skate bowl on his back. His head bounced off the concrete, shooting stars through his brain. Every vestige of oxygen left his lungs, and he lay limp and struggling, seemingly in vain, to suck in some air. At last his chest filled. The inhalation ratcheted pain throughout his body. Were bones broken? Was a bullet lodged somewhere in his torso? Forcing himself to move revealed the answers as no and no.

Overhead and all around him, the quiet was deafening and the darkness blinding. Though he was still clutching the skateboard, his cell phone had flown out of his hand so he had no way to light his surroundings. What had happened to Karissa? The answer to that question was all important. He scrambled onto his hands and knees and pushed the skateboard ahead of him in order to help locate the gentlest gradient to the top of the bowl. His eyes were beginning to adjust to the dimness vaguely eased by streetlights located up the block near a relatively new apartment high-rise.

Hunter reached the top of the bowl in time to see a struggling figure being pushed into the back seat of a vehicle nearby. The door slammed on Karissa and her captors, and the large sedan pulled away from the curb. No matter what happened, he couldn't lose track of that car, and his only mode of transportation was the skateboard clutched in his fists. He half ran, half limped to the road outside the skate park, threw down the board and sent it whizzing after the vehicle.

One of his board wheels was damaged and waffled slightly with every revolution. He probably had that wheel to thank for deflecting the bullet meant to end him. Hunter desperately legged the board to greater speed.

A small transport truck from one of the nearby businesses came cruising past, and Hunter managed to veer over and grab onto one of the slats. The truck, pulling Hunter along, stayed on course with the sedan for a good half mile then started to turn off, and he was forced to release his free ride. Thankfully, the car containing Karissa slowed and turned at the next block, allowing him to keep up. More or less. That wheel was giving him fits now and was likely to fall off at any time. He needed to find another way to stay with Karissa's kidnappers.

A taxi was parked at the curb ahead, but the roof lighting indicated it was off duty. Too bad. Hunter stopped his skateboard and knocked on the driver's window until the guy rolled it down.

"What's the matter with you, pal?" Crumbs of the sandwich the cabbie was eating spewed out his mouth as he talked. "Can't you see I'm not taking passengers right now?"

"I'll let you swipe my bank card for five hundred bucks if you let me in and keep up with that car." He jabbed a finger toward the fading taillights.

"Hop in." A click indicated the doors unlocking.

Hunter didn't wait for a second invitation. He

hurled himself and his board into the back seat. The cab screeched away from the curb. Clearly, Hunter had spoken the driver's motivational language.

"I'd prefer it if you would do what you can not to alert the people in the vehicle ahead that we're following them."

"You some kind of stalker or something?" The cabbie's gaze narrowed on him in the rearview mirror.

"Not hardly. I'm trying to prevent something bad from happening, and you're helping me."

"Okay." The word drawled out of the cabbie's mouth laced with skepticism, but the man stayed on the car's tail—not too close, but not too far back, either.

"You're a natural," Hunter told him.

The guy grunted. "Long as I get my five hundred bucks."

The cars wended their way through Portland into an unincorporated portion of Multnomah County, in the wealthy Forest Park neighborhood that lay just outside the city limits. Rolling pastures and estate-like properties began to displace multihome developments. Under normal circumstances, Karissa might be feeling some nostalgia by now. Hunter may have grown up in Old Town, but this was *her* childhood stomping ground—at least until her parents were killed, and the family wealth turned out to be a house of cards that came tumbling down without dad to keep cobbling it together with the duct tape of financial chicanery.

Hunter had to respect the guts and resiliency that Karissa and Anissa had shown in rebuilding their lives after what must have been a double whammy of devastating blows—the loss of both parents and the illusion of financial security gone in one fell swoop. Oh, yes, the news articles that pilloried Hunter after the fire had also contained these juicy details about the Landon family. If anything, the rich girl–turned–poor orphan angle had deepened sympathy for the Landon twins— one deceased and the other bereaved—and compounded antipathy toward Hunter. Some of the news articles had been downright vitriolic about him, even though his guilt was unprovable and no charges were ever filed. Back then, he'd thought he deserved every word.

In the distance, the car ahead slowed down and then turned into a driveway that led between gleaming white fences. A sprawling ranch-style house with several lit windows sat at the end of the drive. The porch light revealed a sleek limousine parked near the front entrance. Hunter's heart skipped a beat. Were they finally going to encounter the mastermind behind all of this mayhem?

"Stop here," Hunter told the cabbie when they reached the turnoff toward the ranch property. The man complied.

By now, the sedan carrying Karissa had halted in front of the limo, and several figures were getting out, including Karissa, who was then half dragged, half escorted into the house.

"Let me use your cell phone to call the cops." His own cell still lay somewhere at the bottom of the skate park bowl.

"What's in it for me?" the driver said.

Hunter ground his teeth together. He must have drawn the most heartless cab driver in all Portland, but at least the guy had been good at tailing.

"An additional fifty," he offered.

The cabbie tossed his cell over and waited, drumming his fingers against his steering wheel while Hunter, desperately hoping the assignment would reach honest cops, made a terse call about a hostage situation. Surely, the man who owned the limousine didn't have deep enough pockets to own the entire Portland Police Department. Moments later, after swiping the debit card from his wallet for a $550 payment, Hunter exited the cab.

As the car sped away, he hauled in a long, ragged breath. What next? The police dispatcher had told him to keep his distance and wait for the authorities to arrive. What if he didn't have that kind of time before something happened to Karissa and probably Kyle, too?

Sure, Hunter had his gun, but he wasn't about to start a firefight anywhere near a baby. His only other item ready to hand was a crippled skateboard. What could he possibly accomplish with that in the face of armed thugs and a man of deviant brilliance? Whatever it was, he needed to accomplish it fast.

THIRTEEN

"Kyle!" Karissa cried out and ran to the baby.

There were other people in the great room she'd been ushered into, but the child was all she cared about. He sat, kicking and fussing mildly, in the very car seat in which he'd been photographed hours ago. The seat had been placed, facing the room's entrance, on top of a familiar heavy wooden coffee table. This was, after, all, her childhood family home. Almost certainly the scene had been staged to immediately capture her focus upon the baby. The ploy worked, and she didn't care a bit. Not as long as Nikki's son was all right. Karissa knelt and began unbuckling him.

"Leave the child be," an authoritative male voice barked.

Karissa didn't even look around. She'd heard of blind rage before but never experienced it. Until now. How dare these people play deadly games with an infant in the thick of the action?

"If you're going to shoot me, do it," she ground out. "But if not yet then I intend to cuddle this child while I have the opportunity."

"Very well," the voice conceded. "You needn't worry. He's been fed and changed, just not spoiled by carrying him around."

Karissa succeeded in releasing Kyle from his seat straps and wrapped him close in her arms. He ceased fussing and rubbed his little face on her shoulder with a snuffly sigh. Clearly, the little guy craved some comfort and love—things these monsters were ill-equipped mentally or emotionally to give him.

She whirled on her adversaries. If her fury were any hotter, she'd burst into flame—either that or incinerate every being caught beneath her glare. She recognized Scar Lip and Bald Guy. She'd dealt with them before, and they were the ones who had brought her here. They looked a bit worse for wear from the various encounters with Hunter and her. Scar Lip wore a bandage around the arm Hunter had stuck with his knife. The two of them returned her glare with more than a little heat of their own. A couple of other obvious hired thugs, one of them the blond man who had driven the pickup during the abduction attempt in the forest, stood with crossed arms near the far wall. Then there was a middle-aged woman seated regally on the cream-colored sofa near the center of the room.

"Mrs. Hancock," Karissa said, instantly recognizing the pseudo-guide from the Golden Days Care Center, the one who had injected her with something that put her to sleep.

"My maiden name." The woman glared at her, all false perkiness gone.

A faint bruise marred the woman's cheek. Karissa suppressed an unworthy spurt of glee that her defensive fist had likely been the source of the bruise.

A masculine chuckle drew her attention to a portly man of upper middle age and medium height who exuded an air of confidence through gleaming dark eyes and an urbane smile.

"Yes, my wife employed her maiden name during your brief encounter at Golden Days," the man said in silken tones. "Do you recognize me also?"

"Not even a little bit," Karissa responded.

He shrugged his shoulders, creating a small ripple in his tailored suit. "I shouldn't have expected it. It must have been your twin sister who handed me the keys to this place."

Karissa swallowed against knotted throat muscles. "Yes, Anissa handled the liquidation of any family real estate. I arranged the sale of all other assets. We had debts to pay."

"Are you surprised that our game ends here?"

"At this point, little that you could do would surprise me. Clearly, you're capable of any depth of cruelty. I grew up in this house. Your question was intended purely to hurt me. Haven't you done enough of that already? Did you arrange for the truck to T-bone my parents' car? That seems to be a favorite tactic of yours. Did you burn down my sister's house with her in it and ensure she wouldn't be rescued? And I don't even need to ask if you ordered my cousin's death."

The man's smug expression answered her fully.

"But why?" Those two words emerged as an anguished whisper.

"Haven't you yet guessed who I am? I know you must have dropped by the old homestead to pack up before the sale of this place went through and saw something to give you a clue."

A mental picture formed in her imagination: a Realtor's sign in the yard of this property with a slogan on it. Her breath caught as one memory unlocked another—the sight of a realty flyer on the floor of Nikki's cabin near her dead body. The slogan and logo on the flyer was the same as the one on the sign. *Buying or Selling, You Need Marshall Siebender and Associates on Your Team.* Nikki's killer must have posed as a Realtor, and spinning his spiel got him through the front door. Even though Nikki hadn't sounded interested in selling her mountain home when Karissa talked to her, the carrot of enough money would have gotten a pretend Realtor a hearing. No break-in necessary.

Her heart ached at all the loss, not least of all the loss of any hope of exploring her growing feelings for a brave firefighter, especially since he was in no way to blame for Anissa's death. But Hunter was no doubt lying slain, his body not even discovered yet, at the bottom of a skateboarding pit. Her heart tore, and she cuddled the baby closer. This little man she held in her arms was the last person remaining in the world with a familial claim on her heart. Would either of them survive until dawn?

Certainty filled her about her adversary's identity. "You're Marshall Siebender. Anissa told me the Realtor ended up buying our house as an investment. You're... you're...words fail me for how despicable you are!"

Siebender's eyes narrowed to vicious slits. "You should save those words for your father. His actions cost me my daughter and grandson. It's only justice that I should eliminate his DNA from humanity's gene pool."

Karissa's insides curdled. "What in the world could my father have done that was so horrible?"

"For him it was just business." Siebender stalked forward and leaned close to Karissa.

The man's face had gone beet red, and his breath was hot and sour. She gulped and fought the instinct to step backward. No way would she give this evil man the satisfaction, regardless of the way her skin crawled under the fanatical hatred in his eyes.

"For my son-in-law, success or failure in his business was life itself. He tried so hard to prove himself to me—show himself worthy of my daughter. Your father cheated him, ruined him, destroyed him. Three years ago, my son-in-law loaded his family—my daughter and little grandson—into their Lincoln SUV, drove to the Burnside Bridge and—"

"Drove through the guardrail and plunged them all to their deaths," Karissa finished in a small voice.

Siebender drew himself up to his full height and puffed out his chest. "You understood that clue, did you?"

"But I had no idea my father's business practices played any part in that tragedy."

"Of course not, but you're still his flesh and blood that cannot be tolerated on this earth any longer."

"What about Kyle?" Karissa patted the infant's back as he began to fuss again.

Siebender gave that suit-ruffling shrug again. "Still the tainted DNA. I'm afraid you'll both have to go. Don't worry. It will be painless—or nearly so. A neat shot to the head for each of you. So fitting that you should die in each other's arms. Then I'm going to burn this place down over your dead bodies. Here is where it needs to end. Then and only then will justice be fully served."

"But you're wrong about Kyle's DNA." Karissa continued patting the baby's back. "It's my father you blame for your tragic losses, not my mother. Nikki was my mother's sister's daughter. Kyle isn't related by blood to my father's side at all. Surely, you can spare him."

Siebender scowled. "I don't think—"

"I agree with Ms. Landon." The cold-faced woman rose from the sofa. "The final ironic revenge of this tragedy will be that you and I shall claim and raise this child as our own. Restitution for the loss of our grandson."

Siebender's brow puckered. "But sweetheart—"

"No buts, Marshall. *I* want the child. Give him to me."

The woman reached for Kyle, but Karissa backed away from her, earning glaring attention from the thugs in the room who suddenly went on alert.

"I don't know how you expect to get away with this," Karissa spat out. "Too many people are in on the investigation now."

Siebender grinned. "My dear, I already have enough members of law enforcement in my pocket to ensure the investigation stalls out. It will be one of those tragic cases that go cold and all the evidence gets packed into a box and placed in storage."

"Let me shoot her right now," the woman said. "Then

let's take that baby and go somewhere we can enjoy starting a new family in peace."

"Fair enough." Siebender shrugged, capitulating to the woman's demands. "My wife doted on our grandson. I guess her solution makes sense." He sent a shark grin toward Karissa.

Smirking, Mrs. Siebender reached out a hand, and one of the thugs placed a pistol into it. "Now, put the baby in his seat and then hold very still." She motioned toward Karissa with the muzzle of the gun. "I'm not going to miss at this range."

Quaking in every muscle, Karissa took a step toward the car seat even as an enormous crash rang through the room. Karissa flinched.

A battered skateboard rolled across the floor and came to rest in the midst of shards of glass from one of the floor-to-ceiling windows. Every eye riveted on the intrusive board. A large figure leaped through the gap where the window had been and charged like a linebacker into the openmouthed woman with the gun, knocking her flat. The pistol went skittering across the polished hardwood floorboards.

"Run, Karissa!" Hunter hollered as he whirled toward the thugs, fists swinging, even as they grabbed for their weapons.

Clutching Kyle close, Karissa ran.

Hunter's fist connected with a thug's ugly mug, sending a satisfying jolt up his arm. The guy staggered backward and slammed against the wall, then slid down it with his eyes rolling up in his head. What do you know?

He'd scored on a glass jaw. One hired goon down. Three to go.

He went into a whirling crouch as a pair of bullets whizzed through the space where his head had been. He'd had enough of that scar-lipped thug trying to shoot him. Hunter launched himself into a tackle that hit the guy at his knees and brought him down. Hard. But the hired killer was far from out. The man swung at Hunter with the butt of his gun. Bright lights flashed in Hunter's head as the heavy metal bounced off his skull.

Dazed, he rolled away from his quarry—in the nick of time to avoid being shot in the back by the bald goon. Scar Lip didn't fare so well. His leg caught the bullet intended for Hunter, and the guy screamed, dropped his gun and clutched at his thigh.

In a split instant, Hunter's gaze took in the room. No sign of Mr. or Mrs. Siebender, and Karissa and Kyle were gone. That meant he was free to use his own firearm. Grabbing for it, tucked in the waistband of his jeans at the small of his back, he rolled sideways as Baldy took another shot. This one plugged the floor millimeters from Hunter's neck. He returned fire. His bullet didn't miss the beefy shoulder it was aimed at. The quick reflexes of a firefighter and many hours of target practice in the woods were paying off when it counted.

Hunter bounded to his feet as the bald goon went down, releasing his gun, crying out and grabbing at his wound. The fourth hired gunman was darting out the broken window and taking off across the lawn in a dead run. Apparently, the guy wasn't being paid enough to stick around when the going got rough.

Were Marshall Siebender and his wife fleeing the

scene or tracking Karissa and Kyle? Hunter had to assume the latter. That pair had gone to too much trouble and risked too much already to fail in their objective now.

Karissa, which way did you go?

He stepped out through the broken window onto the deck. The night breeze ruffled his hair and cooled his skin but carried no sound of fight or flight. He went back inside to find Baldy and Scar Lip attempting to stanch the bleeding of each other's wounds. They glared at him.

"Cops will be here soon," he told them as he scooped up their guns. "And I don't think they're all on your boss's payroll."

The pair exchanged worried looks.

Hunter left the room and began to soft-foot through the house. It was frustrating not to be able to call out to Karissa, but that would betray his location and hers, too, if she answered.

In the spacious gourmet kitchen, he found the lights were on, and he came across a landline phone with the receiver off the hook. Karissa wouldn't have known he'd called the authorities before he burst in, so it made sense she would try to call for help. He put the receiver to his ear. The line was utterly dead, probably not even in service. Karissa must have been so frustrated.

Soundlessly, Hunter left the room and crossed the tiles of a darkened formal dining room. Moonlight through a picture window allowed him to avoid the shadowy outlines of the furniture. If only he had some clue which direction in this sprawling home she'd taken after passing through the kitchen. For all he knew, he was moving away from Karissa and Kyle, not toward them, but he couldn't stand still and do nothing.

God, help us. The mental prayer sounded feeble to his internal ear.

At least, if he'd overheard correctly from his position outside the great room window while she talked with Siebender, this had been Karissa's home at one time. If anyone would know the best hiding places in this dwelling, she'd be the one. Any slight advantage would be golden in this life-or-death situation. Kyle was the big variable. Would he keep quiet and not give away his and Karissa's location? Highly unlikely. He was a baby doing what babies did.

Even as the thought crossed his mind, an infant's wail reached his ears, faint but unmistakable. If Hunter heard the cry, their enemies had heard it, too. It sounded as if it had come from beneath his feet. The basement!

Hunter whirled and headed back toward the kitchen, one of the most common areas in a house to contain access into a basement. Standing in the doorway between the kitchen and dining area, his cautious scan of the room's interior showed it empty. He began to step across the threshold, but from the shadows behind him a solid object slammed across his back, felling him face forward.

The sharp heel of Siebender's wife's shoe dug into his hand as she relieved him of his gun. Someone else—Siebender, no doubt—removed from his waistband the two other firearms he'd taken from the thugs he'd wounded.

"Up!" Siebender ordered.

Ribs aching, Hunter struggled to his feet. The black

muzzles of a pair of guns—one held by each adversary—stared back at him. Hunter lifted his hands. The gesture of surrender was unlikely to change his fate, but it was the only option he had right now. He mentally prepared himself for the hammer of bullets into his body.

A grinning Siebender tossed away the sturdy chair he'd used to bash Hunter. "Let's adjourn to the basement, shall we?" the man said with mock pleasantness.

Siebender's wife went ahead of them and opened the basement door located on the far side of the kitchen. The sound of a baby fussing drifted clearly up the darkened steps. The wife flipped on a light and motioned for Hunter to precede her downward. Heart hollow and aching, Hunter complied. No matter what they did, it seemed like they lost to these insidiously evil people. That couldn't be right. Yet, here they were, once again in the power of the enemy.

The first area they came to in the basement was large and contained an exercise area on one side, featuring high-end equipment, and a game area on the other, showcasing a pool table, a Ping-Pong table and an air hockey setup. The baby's fussing came from behind the right-hand door of one of two parallel rooms beyond the gaming area. At the prodding of his captors, Hunter forced his feet to carry him in that direction.

He entered the next room and found himself in a plush personal movie theater, complete with cushy leather chairs and an enormous screen that filled an entire wall. Not bothering to pointlessly hide any longer, Karissa scurried out from the half-walled projection booth and ran to him with a squalling Kyle. Hunter wrapped his arms around them, putting his body between theirs and the people with the guns. This was the family he'd always dreamed of having, but their time together promised to be all too short.

"Touching," Siebender mocked.

"At least you'll go together." The wife snickered.

A sound from outside the house arrested everyone's attention. The growing wail of sirens underscored the sudden silence in the room.

Siebender cursed. "My people on the force or the DA's office won't be able to protect us if we're caught anywhere near here."

"It only takes a few seconds to fill these two with holes then we're gone," the wife answered. "Give me the baby." She reached out her arms, gaze implacable.

With a whimper, Karissa surrendered the child and then backed up to stand by Hunter. She lifted her head and gazed up at him. Her eyes conveyed such a wealth of feeling that Hunter's breath left him. Was she regretting as he was that it wasn't likely they'd get the chance to develop their feelings for each other?

"Fall to your right," she whispered.

He complied instantly, taking them down behind the cover of a set of fat theater chairs…but not before a red-hot poker drew a long crease across his back. Several bullets smacked into the wall where they'd been standing.

"Come on!" Siebender cried. "We don't have time to play hide-and-seek. We'll set off the incendiary devices on the way out."

"Right," the wife said. "Are you listening, Mr. Firefighter? Not even you will be able to get out of this one.

We've got it rigged so the whole house will be engulfed in minutes."

Footsteps hurried away, and the theater room door slammed shut.

Hunter staggered to his feet, hot wetness seeping down his back. Only a bullet graze—he hoped. Reaching down, he helped Karissa up. Steel filled Hunter's core. This was not going to end in their deaths. Not on his watch.

"Come on." He grabbed Karissa's arm and pulled her toward the door. Incendiary devices? His gut clenched. "We've got to clear out fast."

Thankfully, the door wasn't locked, since the locking mechanism was on the inside, not the outside. He inched the door open and peered out into the gaming area. All clear. He stepped out, motioning Karissa after him.

In that moment, the pool table exploded, sending burning debris laced with accelerant in all directions. Flaming bits landed at Hunter's feet, and a few stung his bare arms. Nearly simultaneous explosions sounded from various points all over the house. The whole place rocked as if in the grip of a minor earthquake.

Hunter staggered but managed to keep his feet. He turned to find that Karissa had fallen down. He grabbed her, pulled her back into the theater room and slammed the door. His gaze ravaged their environment for an escape route. The good news? Apparently, nothing in the theater room was rigged to explode. The bad news? This room was purposely designed with no windows. There *was* no escape route.

FOURTEEN

Karissa moved to the outer wall of the theater room, coughing as smoke began seeping beneath the door.

"Hunter, over there." She pointed toward a throw blanket that was folded over one of the theater seats.

With a nod, he snatched it and stuffed the cloth into the gap between the door panel and the floor, drastically reducing the amount of smoke that entered the relatively small area. At best, the measure would only delay the inevitable if they didn't find a way to get out of the house.

"What are our options?" Her gaze searched his face as he returned to her.

"I'm working on it," he said, but the bleakness in his eyes told her there wasn't much of anything to work on.

She leaned her head into his sturdy chest. Even though they were once again in a life-threatening situation, his presence brought her comfort.

Karissa lifted her head. "Hunter, I care about you. I—"

Her declaration was cut off by the soft touch of his lips on hers. She closed her eyes and savored the tender sensation. Then it was gone. She opened her eyes to find he had stepped back.

He frowned and looked away from her. "I'm sorry, I just had to do that before..."

"I know." Her words came out soft and breathless. "Don't be sorry. Not for anything. I wish we had more time to find out what might have together."

"Me, too." He shot her a lopsided grin. "But let's not go out without a fight."

"Never!"

"I just got an idea."

He strode over to the side wall near the projection booth, drew up his knee and extended his leg in a flat-footed kick. The drywall cracked and, in the place where his heel had hit, it had punctured beneath the onslaught.

Karissa caught her breath. "Genius! The utility room is on the other side. I almost never went in there, and I don't remember if there are windows or not, but it's a chance."

Hunter grabbed another throw blanket, ripping off two sections. He kept one and handed the other to her. "Tie it around your mouth and nose. Get to the far corner near the screen and hunker down. When this wall opens up, it's going to admit smoke."

Karissa obeyed every word. As she crouched in the corner, sweat dripped into Karissa's eyes, but she blinked the moisture away and kept her eyes on Hunter.

He put on his own improvised mouth and nose bandanna and continued his assault on the drywall, kicking holes in it and ripping chunks away. At last, there was a gaping space between the well-lit theater room and the dimness of the area beyond. As predicted, acrid smoke rippled into the theater room. However, all that stood between them and the possibilities in the next room were some wall studs and electrical wires. Ducking beneath the wires, Hunter squeezed himself sideways between the wooden studs and disappeared from view.

"You were right," he called out from the darkness. "It's a utility room—furnace, water heater, that sort of thing. I can't tell yet if there are any windows."

Karissa had to strain to make out his words with his voice muffled by his face covering and the intensifying roar of the fire outside their door and overhead. The whole house seemed to groan as it was eaten by the flames. Several distinct creaks and cracks sounded from the floorboards above. The ceiling could rain fiery debris down on them any time.

"Come quickly." Hunter's voice reached her ears. "I've found a sink with running water."

Had the smoke addled her firefighter's brain? What was a sink full of water going to accomplish against this inferno?

Nevertheless, she complied, scuttling stooped over beneath the worst of the smoke to the opening between the rooms. Even as she squeezed through into the utility room, the smoke was lessening. How had that happened?

"I soaked the rest of that other throw blanket in water and stuffed it against the door gap," Hunter explained as though he'd heard her question. "A wet barrier is way more effective than a dry one."

He took her arm and pulled her over to a deep utility sink. "Wet your face covering and stay hunkered down near the floor while I continue to try to locate a window. If—no, *when* I do, I'm going to break it with this." He hefted a long-handled broom he must have found lying around. "Be ready to move quickly."

The light from the theater room only pierced the gloom in the utility area about halfway across it. And even that illumination swirled with gray tendrils of smoke. Suddenly, all light winked out.

"We've lost power. Bound to happen sooner or later."

Hunter's voice carried to Karissa's ears as if from a great distance. Was she losing consciousness? In the pitch blackness, the last flutter of hope left her heart.

Then glass shattered.

"Here, hidden behind the furnace. Stupid place to put a window. Follow the sound of my voice."

Coughing, Karissa forced lethargic limbs to obey, but the nearer she crawled toward Hunter's continued calls for her, the more her head cleared. A breeze stirred around her. Fresh air. And a sound besides roaring fire met her ears. Sirens. Right here on the property and more approaching. And light, too. Whirling strobes of red and white poured through a small rectangular window high up in the basement wall.

Strong hands grasped her and pulled her upright.

"I'm going to lift you up," Hunter told her. "Pull yourself out, but be careful for any bits of glass the broom failed to clear from the frame. Ready?"

She nodded then realized Hunter might not be able to make out the gesture.

"Yes!" she cried, joy sending her heart rate into a wild jig.

They were going to make it. The enemy hadn't won after all.

Time seemed to compress as Hunter made a step of his locked hands and lifted her up to the lifesaving opening. With careful hands, she plucked a few bits of glass from the window frame and then pulled herself out into the night. Bitter stench tainted the air from all sorts of burning structural substances, but nothing like the smothering smoke inside. An uncomfortable level of heat radiated down on her from the engorged flames pouring out of the first floor, but the heat and flames surged skyward, not downward.

She stood on the soft grass of her once-upon-a-time backyard. Her childhood home was engulfed, but nothing wrenched her insides about its loss. She'd long ago said goodbye to the place. Now, she waited eagerly for one of the only things she cared about in this earth to squirm out of the death trap to freedom after her. The window wasn't so high he couldn't reach the frame and pull himself up and out.

But no one emerged.

"Hunter!" she cried. "Hurry up."

"Go, Karissa!" his rag-muffled voice answered.

"I'm not leaving without you."

"You'll have to... Karissa, I can't fit through that little window."

His words stopped her heart. She'd known it in the back of her mind as she barely squeezed herself out, but she hadn't wanted to acknowledge the truth.

"Go! Help law enforcement get that baby back from those crooks. You two are the legacy I'm leaving the world."

Sobbing, Karissa ran toward the emergency service vehicles parked in the driveway.

Thanking God, Hunter turned his back to the wall and leaned against it. The outdoor air washed down over him from the window overhead, pushing away the smoke but stoking the fire that had now breached the door of the utility room and was poking brilliant fingers into the dark space, searching for fodder to consume. The cement floor offered no fuel, but the drywall drew the flames. Heat radiated toward him in waves, but fire held no terrors for him. He'd fought it and won too many times. The only instance it overcame him, it had had the unfair advantage of sabotaged equipment. And now he knew that he hadn't been to blame for Anissa's death. He still ached for Karissa's loss of her sister, but his conscience was clear. He could only believe he'd been spared at that time in order for him to come to this moment of saving Karissa. Surely, that was blessing enough for one lifetime.

He coughed as the fresh air began to fight a losing battle with toxic house fire fumes. His legs weakened, and he slid down the wall into a squat. The pain of that motion scraping against the bullet graze on his back preserved his consciousness a little longer.

God, please make sure Marshall Siebender and his wife are brought to justice and Kyle finds a home in Karissa's arms.

The evil husband and wife had to be scurrying to cover their tracks, not realizing that one of their intended victims had survived to tell the story. Probably that was Hunter's biggest regret—not seeing the looks on their faces when they were called to account.

A trickle of something wet landed on his head and dripped down his face. What in the world? He looked up and received a face and body drenching from a garden hose being let through the broken window.

A grizzled male face followed the hose. "Officer Dan Pritchet here," the man said, grinning down at him. "Your girlfriend told us where to find this hose and a hookup from an outbuilding. That water stream won't put the blaze out, but it should hold it at bay until we can knock this window hole bigger with a pair of sledgehammers we've got out here. Go to work, Fireman."

Heart leaping, Hunter struggled to his feet, grabbed the hose and trained the strong gush at the base of the fire creeping toward him. Hissing and spitting, the insidious yellow fingers of heat retreated. For now.

The first blow of a sledge boomed against the concrete of the home's foundation. Then another boom sounded and another in syncopated rhythm as the rescuers went to work. Hunter moved to the side as bits of concrete sprayed inward, soon followed by whole chunks. An ominous creak overhead announced that the ceiling was about to give way. If that happened before they had him out of here, he would be toast—literally—and anyone standing nearby would almost surely be badly hurt or killed by the surge of flames and debris.

"You should get back," he hollered to the guys working the hammers, but it was doubtful they could hear him.

"C'mon, Fireman." Pritchet's face appeared again at the enlarged hole, flanked by another eager male face.

Two pairs of sturdy arms reached in and pulled him up and out onto the lawn. His helpers half dragged, half carried him away from the fire's reach. Through blurred vision, Hunter made out additional officers training the stream of a second hose toward the first floor of the structure right above where they'd dragged him free. Again, not an effective strategy for putting the fire out—a garden hose didn't have the water capacity—but it had been good enough for reducing heat and flames near where the rescuers were working. A sudden deafening crash and a wildly beautiful but deadly bloom of flames signaled the collapse of the interior ceilings into the basement. The officers dropped the second hose and joined them all in scurrying away.

Hunter gasped and coughed as he was lowered to the ground near police vehicles. The distinctive wail of additional sirens closing in told Hunter the real firefighters were about to arrive. Even though the fire department wouldn't even have been called out until the first police units arrived and saw the blaze, the officers in blue would have a heyday razzing the firefighters about showing up late to the party and the police being forced to save one of their own. Or at least a former one of their own.

Where was Karissa?

Blinking through tearing eyes, he spotted her sitting on the ground not far away, being checked out by EMTs. Choking out her name, Hunter crawled over to her on his hands and knees. She broke free of those tending her and collapsed against him, sobbing and shaking, even as Hunter's consciousness faded into oblivion.

FIFTEEN

Fingers entwined with Hunter's, Karissa sat next to his hospital bed and watched him sleep. The volume of toxic fumes he'd breathed in had taken a heavy toll. The extra minutes he'd spent in that basement had worsened his condition considerably. While Karissa had only needed a few hours of oxygen treatment and bronchodilators, Hunter had required hyperbaric oxygenation treatment in a compression chamber, where high doses of oxygen were delivered to his tissues to fade the carbon monoxide from his bloodstream. Thankfully, he was out of danger now and recovering nicely.

With his facial features relaxed, the scarring on the side of Hunter's face was only mildly noticeable. What would he look like clean shaven? She likely would never know—not when she didn't dare stick around to find out. For his sake.

Whoever she loved died and left her behind. Her head assured her that the deaths in her family were due to the actions of twisted individuals, not something destined to keep happening, willy-nilly, if those individuals were stopped. But Marshall Siebender was still out there, posing a threat, and her heart wouldn't be able to risk another loss. Nor could she allow that loss to happen because the one she loved was with her and a target because of it.

Siebender's wife had been apprehended attempting to board a plane to a nonextradition country, but she hadn't had Kyle with her and wasn't saying what she'd done with the baby. Did her husband have him? Karissa shuddered at the thought of Kyle in that man's custody.

At least some of the hired thugs, like the bald guy and the scar-lipped man, had also been arrested. They were singing their lungs out, leading to exposure of a number of officers in police departments around the state, as well as the state police itself—including Detective Sykes and Sheriff O'Rourke. Even members of the Portland district attorney's office, as well as other government offices and personnel in various medical facilities that had done business with him, were getting hit with charges of corruption.

According to the latest update offered to her by a kindly and honest Portland detective, evidence uncovered at Siebender's home and business had exposed a land developer with an operation in bribery and kickbacks on par with a mobster in his own unique good-old-boy style. Overnight, Siebender had made the FBI's most wanted list on racketeering charges, as well as murder, kidnapping and attempted murder, but the man seemed to have vanished from the planet.

The authorities thought Siebender was on the run, probably far from here by now, which was why law enforcement had pulled back on their 24-7 protection of Karissa and now mounted only discreet surveillance on the off chance Siebender popped up. Karissa wasn't as confident as they were that he was fleeing. She'd seen the implacable fanaticism in the man's eyes, up close and personal. That knowledge—that she was still on Siebender's radar—was the reason she couldn't continue risking Hunter's life by remaining close to him any longer.

"Hey, there." Hunter's voice rasped, returning her attention to him.

"How are you doing?"

"Much better, thanks." He squeezed her fingers.

Dropping her gaze, Karissa disengaged her hand from his. Being here when he woke up was a mistake. She was only hanging around in the States, instead of being long gone to Belize, because Kyle was still missing. She had to assure herself the baby was safe, even though the looming threat of Siebender's vendetta would prevent her from applying to adopt him. Once Karissa was gone from the country, Marshall Siebender would have no reason to continue to go after Hunter or Kyle. Well, unless the man held a grudge against Hunter for saving her life numerous times from his murderous plots.

"Don't you dare retreat from me." Hunter's voice had strengthened, and he raised the head of his bed into a sitting position.

"You haven't lost as much as I have," she answered.

What was the matter with her? She sounded bitter. She'd promised herself she would never go that direction. Leaving the country after Anissa's funeral had been a defense mechanism she'd used against the temptation to grow hard and cynical. Or maybe taking off for the mission field after so much family death had been a way of running from emotions she'd never dealt with and burying them under a do-gooder facade. A possibility she might need to unpack and examine at a less stressful time.

"Maybe not as much as you have," Hunter said, "but Siebender's antics have cost me quite a bit."

A lock of his shoulder-length hair fell forward, partially obscuring one of his deep gray eyes. Her fingers itched to brush the thick strand back from his face. She formed fists instead.

"I know, Hunter, and I'm so sorry. I wish I could make it up to you somehow."

"None of this is your fault."

"It's my family sins coming home to roost, so tell that innocence line to my conscience."

"No, *you* tell your conscience you're innocent. I'm familiar with what a miserable, condemning beast that particular invisible organ can be."

She held up a forestalling hand. "This can't be about us right now."

"Why not?"

"Kyle's still missing, and Marshall Siebender is still on the loose."

"Any time now, someone will pop through that door to tell us Siebender is in custody and Kyle has been recovered."

Karissa pressed her lips together and shook her head. "This life doesn't promise happily-ever-after."

"Whatever happened to 'where there's life, there's hope'?"

He reached for her hand, but she stood up and backed

away. "I can't keep endangering you with my presence in your life."

He let out a frustrated noise. "That's ridiculous. I'm with the cops on this. The guy is too smart not to be heading as fast as he can go somewhere that doesn't have an extradition treaty with the US."

"Even if he is gone for now, he could return any time he thinks the heat is off. I've made up my mind. I'm going back to Belize as soon as I'm assured of Kyle's safety."

"Don't you dare walk away without truly talking this out."

"What's to discuss?"

"I get out of the hospital tomorrow. Give me that long. Promise you'll be here when I'm released."

Karissa let out a long sigh. She shouldn't give in. She really shouldn't. But she knew she would. Slowly, she nodded, and the slightest of smiles lightened the dark expression on his face.

When she'd first set eyes on Hunter, she'd been more than half-afraid of his rough and uncivilized appearance. He was big and he was tough and he was brave, a real terror in a fight. He may have come by some of that scrappiness from growing up in the meanest area of Portland, the kind of young man with whom her father would never have allowed her to associate. Somehow that thought made him more attractive to her than ever. But beneath the surface of all the toughness, he was kind, tenderhearted, gentle to the weak and vulnerable, and the most chivalrous man she'd ever known—all contributors to the desperate love she was developing for him. All the more reason to cut ties with him as soon as possible. Her heart was going to take enough damage from this unfulfilled non-relationship as it was.

Yes, walking away was definitely the right decision. If she could bring herself to do it.

Hunter fastened the bottom button on his shirt and cast his gaze around for his shoes. He glanced toward the door of his hospital room. Where was Karissa? She'd promised to be here when he was discharged. He scowled as he located and then put on his shoes.

If that woman thought he was going to let her sudden attack of conscience-driven cold shoulder make him back off, she had another think coming. Of course, he'd bow out in a heartbeat if her retreat from him was due to her genuinely not wanting him around, but he had no doubt she felt their connection and the possibility for enduring love between them. She'd admitted as much in that theater room when the house was burning down around them. He wasn't about to let go of something so precious because of a sick man's threat, and he certainly wasn't going to abandon the woman he loved before she was 100% safe from attack. A thousand of Siebender's ilk could be after her, but she'd still be stuck with him. In fact, all the more reason to stay close.

A knock at the door froze the air in his lungs. Karissa stepped inside, and the oxygen escaped his chest with a whoosh.

"You came."

She tilted her head, brows lifted. "I don't break promises. At least, not if I can help it."

"All quiet for you last night at your apartment?"

"It was. The unmarked police car sat on my street

all night long. I felt sorry for the officers assigned to such a boring stakeout."

"In this case, boring is good."

"Agreed, but one quiet night doesn't mean you're going to be able to change my mind and keep me here. As soon as I'm assured about Kyle's safety, I'm gone. I'm a potential danger to anyone I care about."

Hunter grinned. "I guess that means you care about me."

"Don't get cocky." She sent him a mock frown.

Hunter crossed the room and touched her arm. "I'm concerned for Kyle, too, and I'm not going to stop looking for him until he's found."

"I appreciate that." She offered a weak smile.

Hunter's heart twisted. He'd do anything to bring the light back into her eyes.

"Why don't you let me take you to lunch, and we'll talk about strategies to find him."

She shrugged. "I guess that's the best thing we can do at the moment."

Wordlessly, they walked down the hall together and entered the elevator. Hunter pressed the button for the ground floor. The car started downward then suddenly lurched to a stop. Hunter jammed his finger several times on the ground-floor button, but the car began moving upward instead of down.

Karissa gasped. "Someone has assumed control of this elevator."

"Any guess as to who?" The angry-toned words flew from Hunter's lips.

So frustrating to be caught flat-footed with no weapon whatsoever. Well, except for their wits. They needed to think fast. Hunter's cell phone had been lost at the skate park, and Karissa's had been left at the wealthy friend's house where Hunter had foolishly believed Karissa was safe.

"You haven't by any chance retrieved or replaced your cell phone since yesterday?" he asked her.

"Sorry, no. I was planning on doing that today."

Hunter clenched his jaw. He tried the emergency-stop button on the interior service panel, but as he'd suspected, the elevator unhesitatingly continued carrying them upward. Their panel was clearly being overridden by someone tech-savvy who had all the control as to where this elevator car stopped. They were literally being delivered to their adversary in a box.

"When we stop," he told Karissa, "get behind me as we crowd to one side behind the service panel."

"You've got to stop protecting me. It's me this guy wants."

"I think I've caused him enough grief that I'm fully in his sights, too. If he's got Kyle, we're going to get him back, and I'm not giving you up in the process. You want the little guy to have a loving mother to belong to, right?"

"Of course, but—"

"Then let's do what we can to make that happen. Siebender's tried multiple times and failed to take our lives. Let's keep that score going."

Hunter infused his words with a jaunty tone, but his gut was wound in knots. Other than offering himself as a human shield that would unfortunately fail as soon as he was shot down, he had no clue what strategy to employ next. He was operating on a wing and a prayer. What else was new?

The elevator reached the top level and the door dinged and folded slowly open to reveal…an empty hallway in an area that looked to be under renovation. Hunter blinked to discover no gun barrel staring them down.

"Don't stand there gawking." A familiar voice spoke through an intercom system. "Come meet me on the roof. Let's end this one way or another. Oh, and don't bother looking for someone to help you or try to locate a landline phone. This floor is temporarily closed and utterly vacant. The stairwell to the roof is on your left."

With one arm, Hunter pressed Karissa behind him as he peered out of the elevator into the hallway. A door to his immediate left was labeled Stairs. What was to stop them from scurrying downward rather than up? He found out as soon as he led Karissa through the door.

A rectangular object was stuck to the wall above the landing where the steps went down. Hunter's stomach clenched. A homemade Semtex-based bomb. His firefighter training hadn't included the knowledge of how to defuse them, but he'd been trained to know one when he saw one. If Karissa and he attempted to take the stairs down, he had no doubt that a sensor would set off the bomb. Upward was the only direction available.

Every nerve ending tensed, Hunter hugged the wall as he ascended, and Karissa followed his lead. Her face had gone pale and fear filled her wide, expressive green eyes. Hadn't she been through enough already? A tight fist formed in his chest. Siebender was right. It *was* time to end this.

A metal door at the top of the stairs led them out onto a flat, tar-and-gravel roof. Hunter's gaze darted over the environment, searching for threats. Again, no one and nothing.

Then a portly figure stepped out from behind a chimney, grinning like the fiend he was. Siebender carried a gun, but it wasn't pointed at them, just hanging down at his side like a casual afterthought. Hunter wasn't fooled. If he charged the man, the gun would come up and Hunter would be dead before he could reach his quarry.

"This way." Siebender motioned them toward the low parapet at the edge of the roof.

Keeping himself between Karissa and their enemy, Hunter held her arm as they complied. Siebender moved with them but remained several yards distant. They arrived at the parapet then the gun came up, pointed squarely at Hunter's chest.

"Now, my dear Karissa Landon," the man said, "you are going to jump while your friend watches."

"Why would I do that?" Karissa stepped up beside Hunter.

He resisted the urge to push her back behind him. The steel in her eyes said she wouldn't go. He contented himself with wrapping a hand around her arm.

Siebender smirked. "To save Kyle's life."

"You may have killed him already," Hunter burst out.

"No, I assure you the child is fine and healthy. In fact, he's sitting right over there."

The man motioned with his gun toward the shadow of a vent stack. A tiny figure lay still and quiet in his car seat. Karissa gasped and broke free of Hunter, but he lunged and caught her around the waist before she could escape his reach. He pulled her shaking body close to him.

"Most wise," Siebender said in sync with the click of his gun chambering a round. "The baby is only sleeping, but with any further attempt to dart away I will simply shoot you both. If you don't comply and jump, Ms. Landon, I will ensure that the baby doesn't leave this roof alive."

"You've promised before to spare him if I cooperated," Karissa said, "and every time you attempted to break that promise. At my old home, you would have killed him, too, if your wife hadn't stopped you."

The man's face darkened. "You have yet to truly cooperate. This would-be hero always tags along against my instructions." Siebender waved his gun toward Hunter. "Now, what will it be, Karissa? Kyle's life or yours?"

"What about Hunter?"

"I'm dead either way," Hunter said.

"The man speaks the truth." Siebender nodded. "I can kill him first and then throw you over the parapet. But then I will do away with the child, as well, because you were stubborn. However, since my wife is no longer in a position to raise him, your compliance ensures that I will quietly sell Kyle to a lovely family who is desperate to adopt. Besides, it will be so much more poetic for me if you throw yourself over—with the side benefit for you that you won't have to watch your boyfriend die."

Karissa's gaze met Hunter's. All fear had vanished from her luminescent eyes. Only quiet determination remained. He sent her an infinitesimal shake of the head.

She responded with the tiniest nod. Hunter's insides went hollow. The woman was actually going to do it.

"I'm not afraid of death," she said as she stepped toward the low parapet.

For an eternal moment, her chosen route placed her between Hunter and their cruel adversary. Hunter moved with his firefighter quickness and snatched up a handful of the gravel roofing. Even as Karissa reached the edge of the parapet with Siebender's gaze reflexively following his hated quarry, Hunter flung the gravel into the man's face. Siebender staggered backward, gun discharging. The bullet buzzed past Hunter's ear as he launched himself at the portly criminal.

The pair of them landed hard on the gravel-coated tar, struggling for control of the gun. The older man was surprisingly strong, but youth and size were on Hunter's side. He gripped Siebender's wrist and slammed the man's hand repeatedly on the ground. The man suddenly lost his grip on the weapon. Hunter hopped off his adversary and snatched up the gun then whirled to train it on him.

Siebender was already in motion, charging toward Karissa, who stood, wide-eyed, next to the parapet. Hunter fired and Siebender jerked but still managed to barrel into Karissa. Screaming, the pair of them went over the edge.

"No!" Hunter wailed, racing to the parapet.

With one set of fingers, Karissa maintained a tenuous grip on the cement lip while the rest of her dangled in thin air seven floors above the ground. Flinging aside the gun, Hunter grabbed her upper arm in both hands even as she lost her hold.

"I've got you, sweetheart." He managed to squeeze the words through his tight throat.

Seconds later, he pulled her to safety, and she flung herself into his arms. For a long moment suspended in time, they simply stood and clung to one another. Hunter's heart sang praise to God. Karissa, and also Kyle, were finally and truly safe. He'd seen their tormentor land like a rag doll in the flower bed far below. The man would never hurt anyone again.

"It's over." She sobbed into his chest. "It's really over now."

"Yes, it is," Hunter confirmed, stroking her vivid hair, reveling in the feel of her safe and sound and with him. Where she belonged. "You don't have to leave the country now to keep anyone safe."

Karissa pulled gently away from him and gazed into his eyes. "Do you want me to stay?"

"Of course! More than anything. I want us to find out what we could have together."

"What about Kyle? I mean to adopt him if the courts will agree. Are you okay with a girlfriend that comes with a child?"

"You know it! I wouldn't have it any other way." He grasped her hands in his. "And I'm not looking for a girlfriend. I'm after something way more permanent than that."

One side of her mouth quirked slightly upward, and her eyes lit just as he had hoped they would do. "Do you care to expand on that thought, Mr. Raines?"

Slowly, he sank down onto one knee, her hands still in his and holding her gaze with his own. "Karissa Landon, I love you with all of my heart. There is nothing I want more than to become your husband and a father to Kyle…if you'll have me."

Karissa let out a loud squeal, dropped onto her knees in front of him and threw her arms around his neck. The wonderful, fresh scent of her hair filled his nostrils.

"Yes, oh, yes!" she cried out in his ear then drew away slightly. Her gaze flew upward. "Thank you, God, for giving this orphan a new family."

"Amen!" Hunter responded, helping her to her feet. "I'm not an orphan, so I can hardly wait to introduce you to my parents and my brother, but my heart has always yearned to start a family of my own. How about that? We are each other's answer to prayer."

If his heart were any more full of joy that shoved the recent terror into the pale, he'd probably float away. A sudden infant squawk anchored his feet back to the earth. He had special responsibilities now.

"Kyle," he and Karissa said in unison.

Hand in hand, they walked to where the infant lay in his car seat, kicking and gazing up at them with trusting eyes. Kneeling beside the little guy, Hunter reached out a hand to stroke the baby's soft cheek. Kyle turned his head toward the touch, making sucking motions with his little mouth.

"Hungry," Karissa said.

"Again," added Hunter.

They smiled at each other.

Hunter pulled Karissa close, and their lips met in a long, tender kiss.

EPILOGUE

Nine months later

"Happy birthday to you. Happy birthday to you. Happy birthday, dear Kyle," sang the company assembled around the kitchen table in Hunter and Karissa's Portland home. "Happy birthday to you!"

The healthy one-year-old chortled and smacked his little palms repeatedly on the tray of his high chair.

"Our little guy loves music, doesn't he?" She gazed up at Hunter seated next to her.

They'd been married for four months now, and Kyle was officially adopted as their son. Karissa gazed from Kyle to Hunter and back again, heart expanding fit to burst. How she loved these two men in her life. She was well and truly blessed.

Hunter had never completely deleted his beard, but it was short and neatly trimmed, emphasizing his strong jaw. However, his thick brown hair had been cut to within a couple inches of his scalp. The burn scars on the side of his face were continuing to fade, but she hoped they would never entirely disappear. As far as she was concerned, they were badges of honor.

Hunter met her loving gaze with one of his own and laughed. "I think he's even got rhythm."

Smiling, Karissa wrapped an arm around her husband's strong bicep. Everything about him still gave her that sense of comfort and safety that had helped carry her through so much anguish and danger. She thanked God every day for bringing them together and preserving their lives—especially Kyle's.

As she began to serve everyone slices of cake and conversational banter turned lively, her gaze traveled from one to another of the beloved friends and family who had come to celebrate Kyle's first birthday with them. Of course, there was Buck and his wife, Starla, as well as Jace, Hunter's park-ranger brother, and his lovely fiancée, a police dog handler he'd met during the false alarm at the hydroelectric station those many months ago. Then there were Hunter's parents, a charming and gracious couple who had welcomed her into their family with open arms. Next to them were two of Hunter's best buddies and their wives from the Portland Fire Department, where he now worked as an arson and fire investigator well on his way toward achieving his goal of becoming a fire marshal. And lastly two of her best friends and their families from where she volunteered at the Portland Rescue Mission. What could she say? mission work was in her blood.

She'd also been attending counseling, sometimes with Hunter, but mostly one-on-one to work healthily through her grief issues. However, primarily during these past months she'd stayed home with Kyle, bonding with him and doing her best to be the mommy he deserved. Frankly, he seemed to have emerged from their terrible trial at the hands of Marshall Siebender and his wife with the least trauma of anyone. She thanked God every day for that mercy. Today, his green eyes sparkled, his complexion glowed peaches and cream, and with happy squeals he dug his little fingers into the cake laid upon his high-chair tray.

Later, when the company had left and Kyle had gone down for a much-needed nap, Karissa drew Hunter out on the rear deck of their neat and comfortable rambler home. She raised up on her toes and planted a kiss on his lips.

"What was that for?" He tried to wrap his arms around her, but, laughing, she whirled away from him then turned and sauntered close again.

"You do know I love you," she said, gazing intently up at him.

"I feel the same way about you." The tender warmth in his eyes punctuated his declaration. "But that doesn't answer my question."

"My tenacious husband. Always back to the point." She put a world of affection into her tone. Grabbing his hand, she placed it on her still-flat tummy. "In about seven and a half months, shall we give Kyle a brother or a sister?"

A slow grin spread across Hunter's face. "It's for sure then?"

"It's for sure." She grinned back at him.

"Then I say we are most definitely going to give Kyle a brother or a sister."

Heart soaring, she let him succeed in pulling her close. Their kiss lasted a wonderfully long time.

* * * * *

Dear Reader,

I'm so glad you came along on this adventure with Karissa and Hunter and, of course, baby Kyle. Though everything came out well in the end for them, there were certainly sad times, scary times and hurtful times along the route. In a real sense, that's life for all of us.

The truth is, we struggle with many problems and trials in this world. My hope and prayer for us all is that we walk in that "blessed hope" of Scripture that an eternity of joy in God's presence awaits us. May we be able to express as Karissa did at the end of the story that death holds no terrors for us. Nor should anything this life can throw at us. The apostle Paul was adamant that nothing "shall be able to separate us from the love of God, which is in Christ Jesus our Lord" (*Romans* 8:39).

We cling to promises like the verse above when doubts and temptations assail us and hurtful things happen. Even if we end up the last one in our family, as Karissa did, God is our heavenly family and will provide human connections to warm our hearts and lives. God is, indeed, a good, good Father.

I enjoy hearing from readers. You may contact me by email at jnelson@jillelizabethnelson.com or look me up on my website at jillelizabethnelson.com. I am also available to contact through my Facebook page: Facebook.com/jillelizabethnelson.author.

May your trust in the Lord grow deeper and richer as you read the stories God gives His writers for Love Inspired Suspense.

Blessings always,
Jill Elizabeth Nelson

WE HOPE YOU ENJOYED THIS BOOK!

Love Inspired®
SUSPENSE

Uncover the truth in these thrilling stories of faith in the face of crime from Love Inspired Suspense. Discover six new books available every month, wherever books are sold!

LoveInspired.com

AVAILABLE THIS MONTH FROM
Love Inspired Suspense

SPECIAL EXCERPT FROM

Love Inspired
SUSPENSE

On the run from Witness Protection, Iris James can only depend on herself to stay alive...until a man she thought was dead shows up to bring her back.

Read on for a sneak preview of
Runaway Witness *by Maggie K. Black, available in February 2020 from Love Inspired Suspense.*

Iris James's hands shook as she piled dirty dishes high on her tray. Something about the bearded man in the corner booth was unsettlingly familiar. He'd been nursing his coffee way longer than anyone had any business loitering around a highway diner in the middle of nowhere. But it wasn't until she noticed the telltale lump of a gun hidden underneath his jacket that she realized he might be there to kill her.

She put the tray of dirty dishes down and slid her hand deep into the pocket of her waitress's uniform, feeling for the small handgun tucked behind her order pad.

Iris stepped behind an empty table and watched the man out of the corner of her eye. He seemed to avert his gaze when she glanced in his direction.

A shiver ran down her spine. As if sensing her eyes on him, the bearded man glanced up, and for a fraction of a second she caught sight of a pair of piercing blue eyes.

Mack?

Mack's body had been found floating in Lake Ontario eight weeks ago with two bullets in his back. This man was at least ten pounds lighter than Mack, with a nose that was much wider and a chin a lot squarer.

She glanced back at the bearded man in the booth.

He was gone.

She pushed through the back door and scanned her surroundings. Not a person in sight.

She ran for the tree line and then through the snow-covered woods until she reached the abandoned gas station where she'd parked her big black truck.

Almost there. All she had to do was make it across the parking lot, get to her camper, leap inside and hit the road.

The bearded man stepped out from behind the gas station.

She stopped short, yanked the small handgun from her pocket and pointed it at him with both hands. "Whoever you are, get down! Now!"

Don't miss
Runaway Witness *by Maggie K. Black,*
available February 2020 wherever
Love Inspired® Suspense *books and ebooks are sold.*

LoveInspired.com

Get 4 FREE REWARDS!

We'll send you 2 FREE Books plus 2 FREE Mystery Gifts.

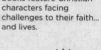

Love Inspired® Suspense books feature Christian characters facing challenges to their faith... and lives.

FREE
Value Over
$20

Love Inspired®

Discover wholesome and uplifting stories of faith, forgiveness and hope.

Join our social communities to connect with other readers who share your love!

Sign up for the Love Inspired newsletter at **LoveInspired.com** to be the first to find out about upcoming titles, special promotions and exclusive content.

CONNECT WITH US AT:

Facebook.com/groups/HarlequinConnection

 Facebook.com/LoveInspiredBooks

 Twitter.com/LoveInspiredBks

LISOCIAL2019